S0-BED-523

Lisa advanced on Joe. "I only hope you can fake it."

"Now, wait a minute. I don't have to fake anything. If you had any doubts about my character, you wouldn't have begged me for this contract."

"If I had another choice," she corrected, "I wouldn't have agreed to help you out. I'm taking a chance on you."

The calculation in Joe's smile sent shivers of warning across her skin. He stepped toward her. "But I'm taking a chance on you, as well. I have to trust you to behave as though you love me."

"You can trust me."

"How do I know?"

"*I* can fake it."

Dear Reader,

This is one of my favorites of the books I've written, because it celebrates the love of a mother for her children. Every once in a while it's nice to remember the sacrifices moms make, which we sometimes don't even know about. The heroine in this story gives her all for her kids. Of course, her efforts lead her to the man she'll come to love, but even moms deserve a treat!

Joe Riley needs to tread carefully with his matchmaking mom until he's reassured of her recovery from a heart attack. Caterer Lisa Meyer agrees to pretend to be his fiancée in order to earn money for a special program for her son. Joe discovers parenting is nothing like heading up a company—it's way more work! So it'll stay strictly business for Joe and Lisa, unless love can find a way.

I hope you enjoy their journey through the intricacies of family relations. I'd love to hear from you. You can contact me through my Web site, www.MeganKellyBooks.com.

Sincerely,

Megan Kelly

The Fake Fiancée

MEGAN KELLY

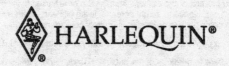

TORONTO • NEW YORK • LONDON
AMSTERDAM • PARIS • SYDNEY • HAMBURG
STOCKHOLM • ATHENS • TOKYO • MILAN • MADRID
PRAGUE • WARSAW • BUDAPEST • AUCKLAND

If you purchased this book without a cover you should be aware that this book is stolen property. It was reported as "unsold and destroyed" to the publisher, and neither the author nor the publisher has received any payment for this "stripped book."

ISBN-13: 978-0-373-75223-2
ISBN-10:   0-373-75223-7

THE FAKE FIANCÉE

Copyright © 2008 by Peggy Hillmer.

All rights reserved. Except for use in any review, the reproduction or utilization of this work in whole or in part in any form by any electronic, mechanical or other means, now known or hereafter invented, including xerography, photocopying and recording, or in any information storage or retrieval system, is forbidden without the written permission of the publisher, Harlequin Enterprises Limited, 225 Duncan Mill Road, Don Mills, Ontario M3B 3K9, Canada.

This is a work of fiction. Names, characters, places and incidents are either the product of the author's imagination or are used fictitiously, and any resemblance to actual persons, living or dead, business establishments, events or locales is entirely coincidental.

This edition published by arrangement with Harlequin Books S.A.

® and TM are trademarks of the publisher. Trademarks indicated with ® are registered in the United States Patent and Trademark Office, the Canadian Trade Marks Office and in other countries.

www.eHarlequin.com

Printed in U.S.A.

ABOUT THE AUTHOR

Fate led Megan Kelly to write romances—fate and her grandmother, that is. While riding a crosstown bus, teenage Megan and her grandma happened on a Harlequin Romance novel. The older woman scanned the first page to determine the book's content and declared it to be about lions, then she gave it to Megan to pass the time on the next day's journey home, five hours away. (The first page did mention lions, but they were statues at the gates of the hero's family estate.) Megan became an avid reader and discovered her dream job—writing those exciting and moving stories she loved. She lives in the Midwest with her husband and two children and is well-known at her local bookstore and library.

Books by Megan Kelly

HARLEQUIN AMERICAN ROMANCE
1206—MARRYING THE BOSS

Don't miss any of our special offers. Write to us at the following address for information on our newest releases.

Harlequin Reader Service
U.S.: 3010 Walden Ave., P.O. Box 1325, Buffalo, NY 14269
Canadian: P.O. Box 609, Fort Erie, Ont. L2A 5X3

For my critique partner, Carol Carson, who nudged me along every inch of this book's journey (sometimes with a cattle prod);

For my kids, who have made their own sacrifices by having a mom who writes;

and, as always, for my husband.

Chapter One

He didn't have time to look for a wife.

Joe Riley stifled his exasperation when his mother cut him off midsentence. She meant well, but her manipulation drove him nuts. He didn't have time for this phone conversation, either. A glance at the in-box on his desk confirmed that. "Mom, I can find my own dates. Stop interfering."

In the heavy silence that followed, the memory of his mother in CCU came into his mind, tubes and machines keeping her alive. He swallowed, pushing away the thought. Trying to be cautious regarding her health, he'd become so indulgent the situation had gotten out of hand—or, rather, out of his hands and into his mother's.

"Ever since I had that heart attack, I've been—"

Joe tuned out her emotional blackmail. He didn't need a reminder of the scare that had made him move to his parents' town just north of Kansas City, Missouri. He did need a plan to stop his mother without upsetting her and endangering her health, and he needed it soon. Last week would have been good.

"And," she continued, "I'm concerned you're heading down the same path as your dad. You work even more than he did. You don't go out and enjoy life."

"You don't have to worry about me." He unlocked his jaw to speak. "I date all the time."

"That's what worries me. You're always dating, never courting."

He laughed. "Courting?"

"You know perfectly well what I mean. You need to settle down. Stop wrapping your work around you at night and get a wife to keep you warm."

"I'm plenty warm, believe me."

"Don't you talk smutty to me, young man."

Joe's face heated. He felt like a hormonal teenager rather than the president of his own firm. "I didn't mean it that way."

"Don't try to sidetrack me, either. I'm going to find you a good woman."

He rolled his eyes. A good woman. Just what he didn't want. He had to do something. Last week, she'd told his secretary she planned to meet Joe after dinner but had forgotten the name of the restaurant. After getting the information, she'd sent the daughter of a friend to meet him. Unfortunately, he'd been closing a deal, not just dining. Besides embarrassing his "date," the incident had jeopardized an important contract. He'd done some fast talking to save the deal and the woman's feelings.

He thought of the women he'd dated in the past few months. Due to the demands of getting Riley and Ross Electronics relocated to the Midwest, too few came to mind. Since he hadn't felt a connection with his dates, he hadn't seen any woman more than once. Work kept him extremely busy.

Desperate sons required desperate measures. Joe took a deep breath. "Look, I wasn't going to say anything yet because I didn't want to get your hopes up. But I guess you've left me no choice."

"You never could keep a secret from me."

He smiled as memories of his teenage years flashed through his mind. If she only knew. "I'm seeing someone. Regularly."

"Oh?" Skepticism laced her tone. "Just how often is 'regularly' with your work schedule?"

"We've been dating for three months. It's not easy to find time to get together, but she's worth the effort. So you don't have to call all the young maidens in the neighborhood. I'm perfectly happy." Joe nodded, pleased with himself. That ought to do it.

"I'm not worried about you being happy, Joe. I want you to be married."

He chuckled. "I have to choose? I couldn't be both?"

"Are you telling me you've proposed?"

He groaned. The woman played hardball. "No."

"So you're not really serious?"

"These things take time."

"How long?"

Joe frowned. He could sense a trap coming, but without knowing what form it would take, he couldn't evade it. "How long for what?"

"How long do you have to date to get serious enough to propose?"

If he could just buy some time to reassure himself about her health… He wanted a wife eventually, just not on his mother's timetable. Once the company got firmly established, he'd enter Wife-Hunt in his PDA under Things to Do. He squinted in concentration. How long had he said he'd been dating this imaginary woman? A couple of months? He was almost certain he'd said two.

"Five months," he said. "Five months just to know,

another to ask her, a couple for her to decide. I'll let you know when it's official."

"What kind of woman takes a couple of months after the proposal to decide to marry you? Maybe your father and I had better meet her."

Joe pulled the receiver from his ear and stared at it. He'd sprung from this woman's loins? No wonder the electronics world considered him a shark. She was cunning and relentless. He couldn't help but admire the trap she'd set.

Still, he had to get out of it. "I can't, Mom," he said. "Work, you know."

"Joey," she said in an understanding tone that raised the hairs on the back of his neck to alert status, "this is why I worry about you so. Too much work. If this girl can't tear you away, maybe she's not the right one. I'll call my—"

"No," he cut in. He didn't want to hear which friend or distant relative she'd call. He didn't want a surprise date at the next family dinner and especially not at his next business meeting. "It isn't just my work, Mom. It's hers. I'm trying to be an understanding guy, you know, respecting a woman's career."

"Mmm-hmm. What does she do?"

Joe glanced around his office, looking for ideas. He pushed aside some papers on his desk. What would satisfy his mother?

"Joe?"

He flipped through some file folders. One had potential. "She's a caterer. She owns the business, so she has a lot of pressure and time constraints."

"What's her name?" she asked with doubt in her tone.

His mother might be convinced if he stuck with his story. He shuffled through the proposals. The hotel would handle dinner, but he'd decided to have dessert trays set up around the ballroom afterward. Pierre, Antoine, Lisa, Caesar— "Lisa. She owns—" he squinted at the paper "—Goodies to Go." He just might accept this woman's bid to cater his company's year-end party out of gratitude.

"Did you say Goodies to Go?" his mother almost purred. "How extraordinary. She's catering our exhibit next week at the Garden Society. I'll have a chance to meet her, after all. Isn't that wonderful?"

Wonderful. The cold steel of her trap tightened around his neck. Knowing he'd stuck his own head in didn't help.

THE DOORBELL RANG.

In the bakery kitchen down in her basement, Lisa Meyer jerked, spurting pink icing across the countertop. Glaring at the chime box over her work space, she wiped her hands and ran upstairs.

She flung her apron on the counter as she passed through the family's kitchen. A quick glance in the mirror had her pushing stray blond hair behind her ears.

Marzipan and icing flowers called her from the basement, taunting her with their lack of completion. She answered the door on the off chance the children might have come home a little early, hands full of leftover pizza boxes. Abby and Bobby were with her best friend, Ginger, eating pizza and playing arcade games—a treat Lisa could ill afford—and weren't due home for half an hour. Hopefully, Bobby had behaved himself and this wasn't them coming home early due to one of his outbursts of temper.

A man stood on her porch, the chill mid-April breeze ruffling his hair. Lisa stared at him, instinctively wary of his good looks. A salesman, no doubt, and probably a good one.

Old Mrs. Winters next door would buy whatever he was selling just to gaze at his attractive features. Tanned skin, hair as dark as midnight, and deep blue eyes. He was tall, with broad shoulders and a body to lust after in a navy pinstripe suit. A light blue shirt stretched over his chest, bisected by a dark tie. If he had a voice to match her imagination, he'd be trouble.

Fortunately, Lisa could resist temptation. Whatever he offered, she had neither the money to buy it nor the time to listen to his pitch.

"Hi. I'm looking for Lisa Meyer."

A voice like roasted marshmallows. She firmly repressed a shiver of delight. "How may I help you?"

His smile widened, carving creases in his cheeks.

She swallowed, wishing she had some extra time and a little spare money. But she had neither, not to call her own, anyway. She straightened her spine and her resolve. "I'm rather busy."

"I don't intend to keep you long. I'm Joe Riley of Riley and Ross Electronics."

Her heart leaped. She'd tendered a bid for his company's function but hadn't expected a personal visit from the president. Thank goodness she hadn't been too rude.

Maybe she'd misjudged him. Just because he wore charm like aftershave didn't mean he had to be a slick conniver like her ex, Brad. Fixing a smile in place, she extended her hand. "Pleased to meet you."

Joe's hand encompassed hers, leaving an impression of warmth and strength. Lisa berated herself. Business, not pleasure, no matter how gorgeous the client. Besides, she'd learned from Brad that a handsome face could hide a devious heart. "Won't you come in?"

She closed the door and gestured to the couch. "Would you care for a drink? Or would you prefer to see my kitchen?"

"A cold drink sounds great."

"I'll be right back." Lisa strode from the room, planning a side trip to the bathroom to do a little primping. She needed to resecure her hair—to comply with health code restrictions, not to impress Joe Riley.

She headed for the kitchen first to get their iced tea. Footsteps on the linoleum tapped right after hers. She looked over her shoulder.

Joe smiled at her. "I thought I'd help."

She shook her head as she retrieved glasses from the cupboard. "This isn't the right kitchen. My business is downstairs."

He walked over to the wall of windows and gazed out at her overgrown backyard while she got out the tea. "I didn't come to inspect your bakery."

"You're welcome to. I'm in the middle of a project right now, but you'll find my set up immaculate."

"I'm sure it is." He turned, and his smile deepened, making those enticing creases reappear.

"I'll show you downstairs after we've talked."

His expression smoothed out, displaying a facade she instantly mistrusted. His eyes remained serious, making him look thoughtful at best, if not downright calculating. Brad all over again, but this time she wasn't blinded by love. This time it was only business. "Shall we sit in the living room?"

Joe took the tray with the pitcher and glasses. Lisa enjoyed the novelty of having someone carry things for her—until he came to a dead stop and she crashed into him. He made a gallant save of the glassware.

"What's the matter?" she asked, moving in front of him. She expected to find a toy on the floor, but the path lay clear.

He gestured toward her refrigerator with the tray. "You have kids."

Lisa glanced at the refrigerator, covered with drawings, baton and soccer reminders, and handcrafted magnets from Abby and Bobby. She didn't understand why her having children threw him off guard. She raised her eyebrows in question.

He shrugged. "I just... Running a business from your home seems more difficult with kids underfoot."

"I based my business at home *because* I have children. It's more convenient and saves money on babysitters. We have strict rules regarding their presence in my bakery."

"I'm sure you do." His gaze flicked to her bare left hand.

Lisa drew herself straighter. "Children, but no husband. Not anymore."

Joe's tanned skin darkened. "I'm sorry."

It hardly seemed businesslike to think of a potential client as cute, but his blush endeared him to her. Lisa led him toward the living room, feeling his gaze on her. Every nerve along her spine prickled with awareness. Settling in a chair across from his, she poured their drinks. She handed one to him and said, "I assume you're considering Goodies to Go for your company's party."

Joe glanced at her, then studied his glass. "Yes, we are. I'm arranging the event myself because I want it to be special. We've had a profitable fiscal year so far, and we want to reward our staff." He took a sip of tea. "A few of them uprooted their lives to follow us from California. Hopefully, the celebration will help our new employees feel more like part of the team."

"I've read about the success of your company. You've created quite a stir in our little town." She raised an eyebrow. "Why did you locate in Howard?"

"My partner, Dylan Ross, is from here. I grew up just east of Kansas City. We worked for the same company in California and became friends as the token Midwestern boys. Later we left and formed our company."

He shrugged. "After my dad retired, my parents remembered Dylan's stories of its small-town charm and moved to Howard. We could relocate the business here because the universities nearby provide an educated workforce. It's small enough for comfort, but not too far from Kansas City to entertain."

"You may have forgotten how precarious summer can be in Missouri, weatherwise. Have you decided on an indoor or an outdoor event?"

He took a long drink. "I'm still looking into both options, although with the humidity, we'll probably opt for indoors. I'll make a decision after I analyze costs." He set his glass on a coaster on the end table. "But I'm actually here today to discuss a different matter."

Lisa's heartbeat quickened, and she eyed him with interest. Did he want her to cater a second party for his company? That would really help alleviate some of the debt Brad had left her. It came to over a million dollars, if she counted the double mortgage on the house, and since the bank counted it, Lisa had to, as well. She needed as much work as she could drum up.

She took a calming breath. Easy, girl. Wouldn't want to appear too eager. "Would this be for your company?"

"Not exactly. Maybe I'd better start at the beginning."

"Okay." She wouldn't get her hopes up, she told herself, but, oh, how she needed the money.

"You're catering the Howard Garden Society's annual show next weekend, correct?"

She nodded, thinking of her frosting flowers in the freezer. The exhibit would showcase hothouse exotics. Lisa wanted her presentations to be as impressive to the eye as they were sweet to the taste. She hoped this commission would lead to others, not only from the Garden Society, whose Rose Exhibit was scheduled for June, but also private parties from the attendees. Word-of-mouth advertising was invaluable.

"My mother is a member," Joe said.

"So that's how you heard of me."

"Not exactly. I got your bid before I knew." He grimaced. "I wish I had known you were catering their event."

He didn't sound happy. What was he, some kind of flower hater? "And why is that, Mr. Riley?"

His direct gaze snagged hers. "Because then I wouldn't have told my mother you and I are practically engaged."

Lisa blinked, then forced a laugh. "You're kidding, right?"

He shook his head.

"But why would you say an idio—" She cleared her throat. "I mean—"

"No, you're right. It was idiotic. I was desperate."

She frowned. "How did I get involved?"

"My mother wants me to get married. She keeps surprising me with dinner partners or arranging dates, then calling at the last minute to inform me."

A man this handsome didn't need help getting a date unless there was something wrong with him, like a felony record he'd neglected to mention. "This may seem presumptuous of me to ask, but since you've involved me in your personal life, I'm going to. Why don't you have a girlfriend?"

He narrowed his eyes, obviously catching her tone. "I'm setting up a business in a new town. I suggested we relocate, moving a thriving enterprise home to take care of my aging parents. I don't have time for a relationship."

"Oh." She shrugged. "Tell your mother to stop."

Joe laughed. Lisa eyed him warily. He thought this was funny? Not that his laughter held much humor.

"You don't know her." He blew out a breath. "She's fragile."

"She doesn't sound fragile."

"My father and I worry about her, especially since her heart attack. The doctor confined her to bed for three weeks." His indrawn breath shook. "She's better now, but not one hundred percent. We have to be careful with her."

While she admired his dedication, Lisa's sympathy went only so far. "What does this have to do with me?"

"She's badgering me to meet 'a nice woman,' and she would have arranged it herself. So I told her I was seriously involved with someone." He gave her a smile and shrugged. "Your brochure was on my desk."

Lisa stared at him, unimpressed with both his predicament and his charming smile. "Tell her the truth."

"I've tried that. She doesn't listen. You're my only option."

A cold weight settled in her stomach. He didn't want her catering talent. He wanted to use her to ward off his mother. Anger warred with disappointment. She'd been right about him, after all. He was as selfish and devious as Brad. Lisa stood, anxious for him to leave.

"Sorry, I can't help you." Her tone came out flat as she realized how much she sacrificed by refusing.

He stood, as well. "You don't understand. She's going to search you out at the Garden Society exhibit and introduce herself to you."

She dipped her head in acknowledgment. "I'm sure I'll be pleased to meet her."

Joe's shoulders drooped. "You're a hard woman."

"Because I won't lie to your mother?" She threw her hands in the air, having had her fill of deceptive men. "Did you think I'd lie to your family in return for this catering job?"

"Hear me out. I'm not hurting my mother. I—"

"Not hurting her?" She stepped closer to him, trying to keep her voice level but unsure she could contain her frustration. "Every lie hurts someone. I don't want any part of it."

"You're overreacting. Let me—"

"You leave my mama alone!"

She and Joe turned as one toward the sound. Six-year-old Bobby stood quivering, his little hands balled into fists. Abby stumbled to a stop right behind him, wide-eyed. Lisa's friend Ginger hovered inside the open front door.

"Bobby, Abby." Lisa reached toward them. "It's okay."

"It isn't either okay," Abby said, sounding younger than eight. "He was yelling at you."

Ginger stepped forward. "Do you want me to wait with the kids on the porch?"

Shaking her head at the offer, Lisa took her children's hands. She needed to deal with this now, to explain about grown-up arguments. Her ex had never argued with her in front of them. He'd just packed his bags and run—with all their money and his new office trainee. She didn't like to think what Brad had been training Lacey to do.

She shook herself back to the present moment. Had Joe shouted at her? She didn't think so. She'd been the one near to screaming. "Mr. Riley wasn't yelling."

Bobby stuck out a stiff bottom lip. "You were fighting."

"We were having a disagreement." She shook their arms

teasingly. "I shouldn't have raised my voice. I sounded like the two of you."

The children glared at Joe from under lowered brows.

"He's a bad man," Bobby proclaimed. He yanked his hand free from his mother's grasp.

"Bobby!"

He ran over and kicked Joe in the shin. Joe grunted and grabbed his leg, hopping a few steps. Ginger covered her mouth, and, knowing her friend's sense of humor, Lisa hoped Ginger wouldn't laugh out loud at the sight Joe made. She glared at her son. "Robert Alexander! We do not kick people. You apologize to Mr. Riley right now."

Bobby pinched his lips together and glanced at her. Abby tried to pull away, and Lisa tightened her grip. "Bobby," she warned him.

"No!" And off he ran.

"It's all right, really," Joe said with an effort. "I can understand how he'd feel, witnessing our disagreement."

Lisa glanced at Abby. Those ever-straying tendrils of fine blond hair stuck to her cheeks. Lisa softened her voice. "Go on up to your room."

The girl stalked away, turning to glare at Joe before disappearing up the stairs.

"I'm sorry." Lisa shook her head. "I hate to say this because I know how it sounds, but they're usually good kids."

Joe's small, tight smile betrayed his doubt. "I'm sure they are. Maybe this isn't the best time to talk. I'll call you tomorrow."

She crossed her arms. "What happened with the children doesn't change anything as far as we're concerned."

He nodded. "I understand. I presented this badly. Let me leave you my business card, and I'll get back to you."

She inhaled deeply. He didn't listen too well, but she'd give him points for persistence. She took his card, careful not to touch him. "I'll accept your card, Mr. Riley, but I'll never accept your deal."

Chapter Two

Lisa opened the door. Joe nodded to Ginger on his way out.

"Hoo-ee!" Ginger gawked after him. "Who was that?"

Lisa rubbed the tension from her temple. "Opportunity, unfortunately. I just lost that huge Riley and Ross job."

"Which one is he?" Ginger's gaze remained fixed outside.

"Riley." Lisa watched his royal-blue convertible pull from the curb then slammed the door. "And good riddance."

"I wouldn't be so happy to see him walk away. Although he did have an excellent backside."

Lisa shot her a wry look. "I'll be sure to tell Kyle you think so."

Ginger laughed. "Like he'd worry. The big lug knows I'm crazy for him."

Lisa gathered up the glasses and took the tray back to the kitchen. She sighed. "There went that. What am I going to do?"

Ginger slid onto the bar stool at the kitchen counter. "Why did he come here to talk to you personally? Your bid couldn't have been too far off."

Lisa grimaced. "I have no idea where my bid was. He came for something else entirely." She poured Ginger an iced tea and filled her in on the details.

Ginger stared out the window, one tangerine fingernail tapping against her glass. Lisa didn't like the calculating look in her friend's eyes. Although her hair fell to her shoulders in apricot waves, Ginger had a redhead's temperament. She was bound to be plotting a nasty revenge for Joe Riley.

"I think you should do it," Ginger said.

Lisa gaped. "What?"

"Seriously, hear me out. You get the R & R job, right?"

"Presumably, but—"

"No, just listen. You get to show off your catering skills. Lots of people find out how great you are. You'll get loads of jobs, and you can pay off more of your debt."

"But I'll have to lie to his parents."

"His relationship with them already stinks, right, if he's doing this? You're not changing anything. You come out ahead."

"Ginger, he's just like Brad. Lying to take the easy way out. Deceiving people who love him. I can't have any part in that."

After a moment, Ginger squeezed Lisa's arm. "Of course you can't. What was I thinking?" She rose. "I'd better get home."

"Did Bobby behave?" Lisa dreaded the answer, especially after he'd just kicked Joe. Bobby's emotions had teetered unpredictably since Brad left eighteen months earlier. Brad hadn't said goodbye to the kids. One night, he just hadn't come home. Only after hours of her worrying and frantic voice mails had he answered his cell phone.

"I'm not coming back," he'd said. Then the phone went silent. He hadn't used it since, according to the investigator she'd hired to track him down.

Another expense she couldn't afford.

Abby had cried for days, then withdrawn, not talking

about her dad again. Bobby had been sure Daddy would come home, but as time passed, his certainty turned to anger. The school psychologist, Mr. Swanson, advised Lisa to let them come to her when they were ready to talk. But "not pushing the subject" didn't seem to be helping either child.

"He was good," Ginger said. "No outbursts. He loved the arcade games."

Lisa went boneless with relief, only then realizing she'd braced herself for a bad report. "Thanks for taking the kids out. I got a lot of flowers done and all my cookies baked."

Ginger waved away her thanks with a distinct gleam in her eye. "My pleasure. It's, you know, good practice to be around them."

Lisa squealed and rushed to her, grabbing her arms. Her friend's smile could have lit up Country Club Plaza for the entire Christmas season. "Are you—?"

"No, but we're trying." Ginger giggled. "Lordy, are we trying. If I'd known how much fun it was to conceive, we'd have started years ago."

"It's not like you haven't had sex, Gin. You've been married for four years."

"Yeah, but now we tangle the sheets with a purpose. Each time, after, we think, 'Was that it? Did we just make a baby?'" She rubbed the bridge of her nose self-consciously. "Dopey, huh?"

Lisa hugged her. "No, it's very sweet and special, like you. Good luck with this."

"We don't need luck," Ginger called over her shoulder. "It's all in the execution. And, boy, can Kyle execute."

THE NEXT DAY, Lisa left off baking early to pick up the children from school. The oven had become temperamental, or perhaps it was Lisa's thoughts of Joe Riley's offer that had sidetracked her, making the cake for the petit fours cook just a tad longer than required. Two batches of cake had been ruined before she noticed the problem. The drive across town, normally about ten minutes, took longer at the end of the school day, as other parents cluttered the roadway on the same errand. She preferred to park and go in to get the kids rather than drive through the pickup lane, so she had to leave even earlier to find a spot.

She retrieved Abby in the lobby, as she was coming back from PE with her backpack all ready to go. They walked down the long hallway toward the kindergarten classes, dodging other kids. Spying Bobby's teacher coming toward them, Lisa smiled. Miss Jensen's mouth turned down at the corners, and Lisa's stomach clenched. Uneasy about the answer, she asked, "What is it?"

"Fighting. He's in the principal's office."

Lisa closed her eyes. "And I was having such a great day."

"We sent home a note yesterday. I guess you didn't get it since it didn't come back signed today."

Lisa's jaw dropped. "What happened yesterday?"

"He pushed another boy, and we have a zero tolerance policy regarding any show of violence. He spent thirty minutes working in the hall. The other boy called Bobby names. I don't know the details, as neither would tell me." She sighed. "Today, Bobby hit the child. Arnold's nose isn't broken, but it bled a great deal."

Lisa swallowed.

"Bobby appears to have gotten the worst of it," Miss Jensen said, as though that counted in Bobby's favor.

The principal's secretary opened the door and gestured

them in, forestalling any comment. Lisa turned to Abby. "You stay here."

She stepped in and then froze as she saw her son. When she gestured for him to show her his face, he lowered the ice pack. "Oh, my God." He had indeed gotten the worst of it, if that was Bobby under the swollen cheek and purple eye.

"We were about to call you," said the principal, a smarmy-mannered chauvinist who always scraped Lisa's nerves. "But the incident occurred right before dismissal."

Lisa wanted to pull Bobby to her and rock him, showering him with kisses. *The incident?* Where was the teacher when some bully was beating her baby? She turned to Miss Jensen, forcing herself to remember how much she usually liked the young woman. "How did this happen?"

Mr. Bushfield cleared his throat. "Maybe we'd better ask young Robert that."

Lisa locked gazes with her son. "I fully intend to talk to Bobby."

Bobby grimaced, then winced and replaced the ice pack.

Bushfield held up his hand. "We expect our young people to own up to their mistakes. We prefer them to take responsibility for their actions." He paused. "Of course, you must handle this however you think best."

Lisa gritted her teeth. His implication hung in the air. She wanted the teacher's version because she didn't trust her own son to tell the truth. The guy was a jerk. She turned her back to him. "Miss Jensen?"

"Bobby hit Arnold." She shook her head. "By the time I got across the room, Arnold had slammed Bobby to the floor. I didn't see how it started."

Lisa would have to find out what happened from Bobby, after all. She hated to give Bushfield the satisfaction. Dying to ask about punishment for this Arnold kid, Lisa said with forced politeness, "How is the other child?"

"His parents are coming from work," Miss Jensen said, "so he's waiting in the nurse's office. His nose has stopped bleeding. I'm sure he'll be fine."

Taking Bobby's hand in hers, Lisa faced the principal. "The question of 'why' will have to be settled later."

"He must—" Bushfield blustered.

Lisa raised her chin and reached for dignity. "The real problem is that it happened at all. What discipline measures does the school enforce?"

The administrator gawked, clearly two beats behind and trying to catch up. "What do you mean?"

"Is he suspended? Do kindergartners serve detention?"

"We've found detention to be ineffective as a discipline tool for this age group. The child's self-esteem can be severely damaged."

Lisa exhaled slowly so he wouldn't notice she'd been holding her breath. "I agree. I would recommend against suspension, as well. Bobby will learn more by facing Arnold and their classmates than by staying home."

Bobby scowled then readjusted the ice pack.

Bushfield wiped his pudgy face. "This mustn't happen again."

"It won't," Lisa assured him.

He leaned forward and shook his finger in Bobby's face, a looming figure in his dark suit. "This will be on your permanent record, young man."

Miss Jensen uttered a soft protest. Lisa pushed Bobby behind her.

"It does little good to protect him," Bushfield said.

"Good day." She restrained the urge to slam his door.

"Ms. Meyer," he called out just before she could escape. "There is an alternative program I've been considering for young Robert."

Lisa stopped. If he mentioned juvenile detention, she would smack him. She swallowed a grin. Maybe the air in the school turned the Meyer family into violent reactionaries. "Bobby, wait outside with your sister."

Bobby scooted around her into the secretary's office.

Abby gawked at his face. "Cool."

Lisa glared at them both before stepping back in and carefully closing the principal's door. "What program?"

"In my opinion, Bobby is bored with school, and this is why he's acting out."

Lisa tried not to roll her eyes. Acting out. Sheesh. In her opinion, this Arnold kid had goaded her son, and Bobby had "acted out" with his fist. His problem stemmed from his anger at his father.

"Have you spoken with Mr. Swanson?" she asked, referring to the psychologist. She'd endured team meetings all year with Bobby's teacher, principal, the school psychologist and the social worker, appreciating their concern for her son, even though she didn't always agree with their assessments. Bobby met with Swanson every week, trying to talk through his feelings toward Brad and formulate ways to curb Bobby's outbursts of temper. Anger management for a six-year-old. Lisa felt like such a failure as a mother.

Bushfield nodded. "He sees the merit in my suggestion. Unfortunately, he had another meeting after school today. We could wait until he's available to discuss this, but I would hesitate to detain any help for Robert, given recent circumstances."

Lisa turned to his teacher. "I thought this disagreement

only happened yesterday and today. Is he fighting with other kids, too? Have you had other problems with Bobby?"

"Not fighting, no," Miss Jensen said, "although I have noticed how withdrawn he's become since Christmas. He doesn't interact with the other students, usually preferring to read rather than play with them."

"Withdrawn?" Lisa's mouth went dry. He'd expected his dad home for Christmas, but they'd talked about it and she thought he'd accepted it. She hadn't realized the depth of his disappointment. When had Bobby quit playing with his friends? He loved to join in any type of game. How had she not known? Of course, she only came to school on special party days. She'd thought his outbursts of anger were his only problem.

"In the program I'm suggesting," Bushfield said, "the children meet with instructors before and after school to study art, music and a foreign language, as well as participating in some recreational activities to challenge their bodies as well as their minds. We, of course, offer breakfast and an after-school snack to keep their energy levels high."

"Bobby doesn't need day care, Mr. Bushfield."

"But he needs challenge, Ms. Meyer. One of the problems with Bobby is that he's brighter than his classmates. We can't advance him into first grade this late in the school year."

Lisa pushed down a surge of maternal pride. Of course, she considered Bobby brighter than average but felt gratified to hear it from educators. Why hadn't they noticed how intelligent Bobby was before this? Shaking her head, she knew the answer. In their overgrown school district, only the special needs children got particular attention. The ordinary kids who didn't struggle academically or misbehave were overlooked.

Before, Bobby had been evaluated as troubled. Now with the fighting, her son would be labeled a problem child. Smart, they could ignore and plan extra work for the next year maybe. Disobedience and fighting, however, had to be addressed immediately.

"With only weeks left in the school year," she said, "I wouldn't want you to move him. How will before- and after-school 'challenges' help him behave during class?"

Bushfield opened his mouth but offered no answer before closing it again.

"And," Lisa continued, "his temper problems aside, today's 'incident' sounds like a personality conflict between Bobby and this Arnold kid."

"If my son were fighting," Bushfield said, "I'd be concerned."

Pompous ass. Lisa reached deep inside herself for patience. "I am concerned, Mr. Bushfield. I just don't agree that this is the answer for Bobby."

Bushfield leaned back in his black leather swivel chair and linked his fingers over his paunch. "We considered this program for Bobby in the fall because of his abilities, not because of his misbehavior."

Her teeth clenched so tight her jaw ached. His misbehavior? What about that other kid, calling Bobby names and smashing his head on the floor?

"However," the principal continued, "this opportunity cannot be offered to every child due to its cost."

The blood drained from Lisa's face. Because she'd had to sign up for reduced lunch prices and book-fee assistance for both children, all her financial information lurked in the kids' files. No doubt Bushfield and every other administrator had access. It was degrading.

Now it came down to money again. Bobby hadn't been considered last fall because she was broke? She swallowed her rage. Damn Brad.

"Unfortunately," the principal continued, "it isn't funded through tax revenue, and we must rely upon the parents— or parent in your case—to provide the majority of the tuition. Bringing highly talented professionals together to educate our children with the best cultural activities is expensive." He cleared his throat. "Given that Bobby's special needs have intensified this week, we might be able to provide a grant through the school district for the remainder of the year. Some monies have become available."

Lisa tried to remain expressionless. Humiliated beyond measure because she couldn't afford to give her child this special opportunity, she fought her anger—against Bushfield, against Brad, against anyone she could think of, especially herself. No way would she allow her children to suffer because she had been left with an overwhelming debt. If only that investigator could track down Brad, perhaps she could squeeze some child support from him. Unfortunately, rumor had it Brad had left the country.

She stiffened her spine and eyed Bushfield steadily. "If you have a brochure, I'll look it over."

She marched out with her head held high, determined to get the money somehow, even if she had to sell her soul to the devil.

Fortunately, she'd just met the devil. He was handsome and devious, and he needed a favor from her.

Chapter Three

The next day, Lisa paced the waiting area outside Joe's office, recalling her adamant refusal to help him. Now she had to swallow her pride and ask for a favor. She could humble herself for her children. She'd had practice enough in the past eighteen months. But deceiving Joe's parents stuck in her craw.

Unfortunately, she didn't have much choice. She wanted to rise above the humiliation of being broke, but more importantly, she had to get Bobby into that program. Providing for her children drove her every action.

The night before, Lisa had seated herself beside Bobby as he climbed into bed. She brushed a stray lock of white-blond hair off his forehead.

"Bobby, why did you hit Arnold?"

He stared at his lightweight blanket, threading it between his fingers. His shoulders rose and fell in a shrug.

The cicadas started their nightly song outside. An early June bug thunked against the window screen, trying to reach the light. The overhead fan whirred. Her son said nothing.

She bit her bottom lip, then prodded, "Bobby? You must have had a reason."

Still not looking at her, he mumbled, "He called me a name."

Lisa sighed. She'd gotten that much from his teacher. "Honey, you can't just hit people because you don't like what they say. Miss Jensen said you shoved him yesterday, too."

He shrugged again.

"And you kicked Mr. Riley."

Bobby's eyes flashed to hers. "But he was yelling at you!"

"No, honey, he wasn't. Even if he had been, it would still be wrong to kick him."

Bobby's bottom lip stiffened. "I'm the man of the house now. Just like on TV."

Lisa's chest tightened. How could she scold him for protecting her? She kissed his forehead. "I love you. But no more hitting, no matter what the reason. Hitting doesn't make a boy into a man."

He didn't respond, but Lisa knew he'd heard her.

Now she glowered at Joe's pretty young secretary, who kept her gaze on her computer monitor. The brunette might appear to be a bubblehead, but she'd guarded Joe like a pit bull, not letting Lisa speak to him. Lisa had hoped to make this distasteful arrangement on the phone or at her house, giving her home-field advantage. But Joe's secretary screened his calls and relayed his messages, limiting her access—no doubt on his orders. He could only fit Lisa into his schedule if she came to see him that morning. Given Bobby's increased violent streak, the sooner she received the advance money and could enroll him, the better.

"Lisa." Joe's deep voice shivered through her. He leaned against the door frame of his office, hands in his pants pockets. "I must admit I'm surprised to hear from you, but I'm very pleased."

He radiated confidence, with a touch of smug victory. In

a dark charcoal three-piece suit, he looked even more handsome than she remembered. Her mouth went dry. Nerves, not attraction, she assured herself. She nodded cordially. "I'd like to discuss something with you."

A second man emerged from Joe's office, sans jacket or tie, with his gray shirt unbuttoned at the throat. Dark blond hair brushed his collar.

"This is my partner, Dylan Ross," Joe said. Turning to Dylan, he added, "This is Lisa Meyer, owner of Goodies to Go. We're about to negotiate the fine points to her providing desserts for our first fiscal year-end party in Howard."

"Nice to meet you." Dylan stepped forward and shook Lisa's hand.

"Are you staying for the meeting, too?" She darted a look at Joe, relieved when he shook his head. At least he hadn't spread the tale of their distasteful pact.

"Sorry," Dylan said, a teasing light in his blue eyes. "Joe conveniently forgot to mention how attractive the caterer was he had to meet with. How'd you let that happen, Sue?" he asked Joe's secretary, who watched their exchange avidly. Dylan glanced at his wristwatch. "Come to think of it, I might be able to spare a few minutes."

"No, you really can't." Joe took his arm and marched him a few steps on his way.

"See you again," Dylan called with a laugh as he continued on his own steam toward the door.

"Nice to meet you." Lisa was still smiling when she met Joe's narrowed gaze.

"So you've reconsidered?"

She glanced at his secretary, who bent over her keyboard, actively not listening. "Under certain circumstances, I might agree to your...proposition."

Joe smiled. "I'm intrigued. Shall we step into my office?"

Said the drooling wolf to the lamb. Not fooled by his charming facade, she ignored the warmth of his hand on her elbow, as well as the tingle chasing through her blood.

Lisa couldn't decide what to make of his enormous office. Neutral colors and light wood tones blended into blandness. Dark glass in the windows cloaked the sunlight. No plants to add life; no photographs graced his desk. Although tasteful and professional, Joe's office presented an impersonal face to his associates. It certainly chilled her.

"Thanks for meeting with me here," Joe said after seating her on a tan leather sofa. He settled in one of the three chairs across from her. "Would you care for a drink?"

Lisa declined with a shake of her head.

"Perhaps I could take you to lunch afterward?"

She smiled with insincere sweetness. "That won't be possible. I had to rearrange my morning to suit yours. I have work to complete this afternoon."

He chuckled as she evened the score.

"The flower show *is* in four days, you know."

He winced. "I remember."

Lisa almost crowed with satisfaction. She had him. He'd have to agree to give her the contract.

"You said you'd help me under certain conditions." Joe's manner turned less personal. "I assume you're talking about catering our company party."

"Yes, but that's not the cond—"

He held up his hand. "I assure you I didn't mean it as a bribe at the time, and I don't think badly of you for agreeing to it now. It's just a—" he waved his hand vaguely "—an exchange of services."

Lisa bit her lip. For two cents, she'd walk out and leave

him hanging—for two cents and about half a million dollars, which she didn't have. Joe might need her to extricate him from this tangle of lies he'd woven, but she also needed him.

Dammit. She'd worked her rear off whittling down that debt. They'd still have to live hand-to-mouth for a while, but she had started to rebuild her life. Maybe in a year or two she could get a credit card, although it would no doubt be a prepay deal. But to have a credit rating she could be proud of. To pay off her business loans. To take her children to the pizza place herself and not cower at the cost of the arcade games. Oh, she'd do a lot for that. She'd enroll Bobby in that enrichment program, then stuff the check for the whole amount, without any grants from the school district, right up Bushfield's nose.

She took a deep breath. "First, let me assure you I wouldn't do this if I could come up with another solution."

Joe's eyebrows rose.

"I stayed up all night, worrying over this. If there was any way not to have to make this deal with you, any way at all…" She clenched her hands together.

"Is this your way of asking me for a favor?"

Lisa's face heated. She'd insulted him. Not a promising start. Rubbing her temple, she mentally altered her phrasing. "No, it's my way of proposing a deal. I believe in honesty, and although I might agree to your deception, it goes against my nature. I want you to understand my desper—my position."

Joe leaned toward her. "Go on."

"You need me to pretend to be your girlfriend, to appease your mother. I need your catering contract, but I don't want our arrangement to upset my children. My condition is simple. They're not to be involved. You're not to be around them. It's out of the question."

He studied her in silence. After an eternity, he said, "I don't see how I can stay away from the children since we'll be dating." His tone laced charm with silken warning.

"I thought I'd just meet your parents once or twice. At the Garden Society exhibit and maybe one other time in a couple of weeks to cap off the pretense."

He shook his head. "We'll have to be seen out together. My mother has a network of friends. She wouldn't believe we have a serious relationship if we aren't spotted around town. We're supposedly on the brink of getting married."

Lisa sighed, conceding his point. "Fine, but no meeting the kids. They're a little confused right now, basically due to their father's desertion. Brad, my husband, wasn't… He didn't…"

She jumped to her feet, unable to stay still.

"It wasn't an amicable divorce?" Joe asked.

She snorted, then caught herself and paced away. "No, it wasn't. It's been a year and a half of upheaval for the kids." She leaned back against his desk and gazed into mid-distance between them as some of those upheavals ran through her mind. The children's tears. Her shock at sudden bankruptcy. Their nightmares. Their confusion and hurt.

"Is there any chance you and your husband might—?"

"No." She shuddered. Not even for the children.

Joe nodded. He tapped steepled fingers against his full lower lip. Lisa ground her teeth, both irritated at him for his relaxed position while her world teetered to disaster, while also impatient with herself for noticing his seductive mouth at such a time.

"So what am I supposed to be?"

She swallowed another lump of pride and confessed, "You're the provider of a contract that'll bail me out of a financial bind."

"No, I meant what will your children think I am to you?"

She stared at him. Having forced herself to admit she needed money so badly, she couldn't switch tracks fast enough to follow his train of thought.

"Am I posing as your lover or whatever the kids would call it?" His mouth twisted. "Your boyfriend, I suppose."

Lisa snapped her mouth closed. "No, that's not what I'd planned, at all. I thought you could just be my client."

Joe stood and walked toward her.

She forgot how to breathe.

"I'll be picking you up for dates, for my parents' sake, remember? Your children will know we're more than business associates."

"Not…not if I explain that I'm doing you a favor."

His smile was less than nice. "But you're not going to explain that to them. You're not going to explain it to anyone. Word gets around. Kids tell kids, who tell parents, who might know me or my folks."

"Oh." Her pounding heart impeded her thinking. She couldn't breathe; she couldn't think. Maybe being around Joe wasn't such a great idea.

"It's our secret. You're my girlfriend, lover, or whatever you want to call yourself."

"Girlfriend," she interjected, shying away from the thought of being Joe's lover.

"Fine." He leaned so close his cool breath brushed her lips. She inhaled his male warmth. His gaze held hers. "My parents will consider us almost engaged. We don't tell anyone the truth." His low voice compelled her to agree. "We pretend to be madly in love with each other. Understand?"

Compelling was one thing; intimidating was another. She simmered. Who did he think he was? She'd put up with too much garbage in the past eighteen months to be pushed around by Joe Riley.

She locked her gaze on his. "I understand perfectly. Do you understand you have to pretend to be honorable when you're around my children?"

He straightened, blank surprise on his face.

"Can you keep your real character a secret?"

"What are you talking about?"

Lisa advanced on him. "Your tendency to lie your way out of trouble—"

Joe backed away, his hands up to ward her off.

"Your attempt to bribe me." She stepped forward. "Your—"

He stepped back. "Now wait a minute—"

"I only hope you can fake it."

He halted. "I don't have to fake anything. If you had any doubts about my character, you wouldn't have begged me for this contract."

"If I had another choice," she corrected, "I wouldn't have agreed to help you out. I'm taking a chance on you."

The calculation in Joe's smile sent shivers of warning across her skin. He stepped toward her. "But I'm taking a chance on you, as well. I have to trust you to behave as though you love me."

"You can trust me."

"How do I know?"

"I can fake it."

He smirked. "I've never had a wom—"

"Don't even say it."

"Maybe I ought to put you to the test."

She eyed him with suspicion. "What test?"

"We'll be performing in front of my mother, who can sniff

out a fraud like a bloodhound." He smiled. "Maybe we ought
to rehearse."

"What? Why?"

"We're not exactly friends. My mother—everyone—will
be able to tell if it's our first kiss. We should practice, just
until it feels natural."

Lisa glared at him, disgusted with his tactics. Another
manipulator, just like Brad. "I should've expected something like this from you." She stalked to the door, followed
by Joe's laughter, soft, but edged with triumph. "Mail me
the contract."

"Coward," he called across the room.

"*With* the advance money." She slammed the door on his
grin.

LISA TOOK HER CHECK to the principal's office the next day
as school let out, Joe's advance having arrived by special
courier. Laying down the money for Bobby's program,
without having to apply for any grants from the school
district, didn't offer her the satisfaction she had imagined.

Abby jumped into the car. Bobby had been invited to
practice soccer at the house of one of his teammates.
Tomorrow she'd tell him about his starting "a new adventure," which was how she'd decided to view the program.

Lisa hated to cut into her special time alone with Abby
doing a mundane chore, but she needed to stop at the
grocery store on the way home. Time seemed to slip away
from her these days, never leaving enough for all the things
she had to do.

"Sally Turner's having a birthday party, Mom, and she
invited me! Everyone's going. Can I go? Please."

After an affectionate glance at Abby, Lisa checked the

rearview mirror for oncoming cars then pulled into traffic. "When is it?"

"Her birthday is next week, but the party's not till June eighth. It's a Sunday. We have lots of time to shop."

"What are you planning to get her?" She could stretch the budget to include a present, as long as Sally "The Girl Who Has Everything" Turner didn't expect expensive name brands. "Why is her party so far in the future?"

"Everybody who's invited decided to get new T-shirts with the band's name on them. I can have one, too, can't I? It shouldn't cost too much."

Lisa frowned. "What band?"

"Oh, I forgot to tell you the best part!" Abby bounced on the seat in her excitement, a grin splitting her face. Lisa hadn't seen her this happy or this animated since Brad left. *Thank you, Sally.*

"Sally's parents are taking us to see Juniper Jones."

"Wow." Concert tickets for the Turners and a group of girls would cost a load of money. Lisa bit her lip, hoping Abby understood her own birthday celebration wouldn't include anything nearly as expensive.

"So I can go?" Abby insisted.

"I suppose so."

Juniper Jones was the name of an all-girl band, whose songs focused more on friendship and teen angst than drugs or sex. Abby had their two most recent CDs, and their poster decorated her wall. At least the Turners, whose lax parenting methods Lisa usually abhorred, had chosen music appropriate for eight- and nine-year-olds. She struggled over letting them take her daughter to the crowded concert. Surely they could be responsible for Abby for one evening.

"That's really cool," Lisa said. "I didn't know Juniper

Jones was playing in Kansas City this summer. I suppose we can find a band T-shirt somewhere."

Maybe one of those Internet bargain sites would have a shirt available. Souvenirs at the concert were costly.

Abby hunched in her seat. "They're not."

Sure she'd lost track of the conversation, Lisa said, "I don't understand."

"We're going to see the concert in St. Louis. We get to stay overnight at a hotel. With a pool."

Fortunately for the other drivers on Wilson Avenue, the light ahead turned red. Lisa braked with extra care then stared at Abby. She wouldn't even let parents she trusted take Abby across the state overnight, let alone the Turners. "And you're just now mentioning this part."

Abby nodded, not quite meeting her eyes.

"After you made sure I said you could go." Lisa tightened her grip on the steering wheel. "I'm sorry, Abby. The answer's no."

"Mom!"

She raised an eyebrow at her daughter, a definite warning sign should Abby care to heed it.

Abby's chin dropped onto her chest. "That's so unfair."

Lisa inhaled and glanced ahead. Still red, thank heavens. She didn't think she could negotiate traffic and this conversation without killing someone. Preferably Sally Turner's parents. What were they thinking? She shook out fingers gone numb from her hold on the steering wheel.

The light changed, and Lisa carefully advanced.

After three blocks, Abby burst. "Why can't I go?"

Lisa let the silence hold until she parked at the curb in front of the store. "It's too far. You can't stay overnight in another city at your age without me."

"Sally's parents will be with us. And it'll be summer, not a school night."

Lisa held up her hand. "Don't start. You knew what the answer would be before you asked, which is why you wanted me to say yes before you filled in all the details. I don't appreciate being manipulated, young lady."

"Sorry," Abby muttered.

Lisa blew out a deep breath.

They got out of the car, although Lisa had never felt less like seeing food in her life. Abby got quieter as the hours progressed, and by bedtime, Lisa almost wished the girl would let loose her feelings the way Bobby did. Abby's silent melancholy tore at her heart.

AT THE CONVENTION HALL the next week, Lisa glanced around at the hothouse exhibit of roses, orchids and gardenias and felt satisfied that her sugary confections complemented the beauty of the room. Moreover, her flowers offered a delight for the tongue as well as the eye. About fifty women in sequins and chiffon led their handsomely suited men through the partitioned-off areas. Muted conversations, briefly punctuated by outbursts of greetings, blended with the classical music in the background.

Lisa darted to the main dessert table to inspect the platters again, having checked on the four satellite stations she'd set around the room. She felt the eyes of the attendees drifting over her. Eager to make a good impression in hopes of future business, she smiled at everyone and said a few words, while trying to maintain a professional, I'm-just-the-invisible-help type presence.

"I need to set out more cookies," Ginger said as she replaced a tray of mint crème candies. "Things are going really well." She laid out more cocktail napkins and plates then whisked her tray to the next table.

As Lisa gathered up the dirty dishes and hurried toward the convention hall's kitchen, the hairs on her neck prickled. *She* was here someplace, poor Mrs. Riley, hoping to meet Joe's "almost fiancée." Lisa swung through the metal kitchen doors, making sure they swished closed. Shame filled her as she imagined her upcoming performance, duping that fragile old woman into believing her son's happiness was assured. Tricking Mrs. Riley in her last days would secure Lisa a long stay in purgatory.

She dumped the dishes on the stainless steel counter and wiped her forehead with the back of her wrist. The hall's kitchen made her salivate with envy. Cool, smooth metal expanses of countertops, an industrial-size fridge, two freezers, three ovens…

Lisa reined in her yearning. She didn't need this much equipment, not for her simple operation. The scope of the night's party had been huge enough. Even with Ginger's assistance, getting everything here and setting up had depleted her enthusiasm for catering large jobs. She should have hired more servers, but she simply couldn't afford them. Ginger had offered her help for free, but Lisa insisted on paying her.

She couldn't bring herself to take anything more from anyone. In addition to paying back loans from half the banks in town, she had to repay Joe Riley. With her affection.

The back of her right eyeball cramped.

Deceiving Mrs. Riley into thinking she loved Joe would take an acting job worthy of an Academy Award. No wonder she felt a migraine intensifying.

Ginger backed through the large swing doors into the

kitchen, her arms laden with a tray of dirty dishes. She set it on the worktable and guzzled a drink from her water bottle. "Wow, they really love your stuff. I bet you get tons of catering calls after tonight."

"I hope so," Lisa said. "Don't worry, though. If I do, I'll hire some college kids to help out."

"It's kind of fun. Although it is harder than trying to make a baby, which is what I have to get home to do." She referred to her fertility cycle, a timetable for conception she and her husband called the Baby Project.

Lisa glanced at her watch. "Oh, Ginger, go on ahead. Kyle should be home from his meeting by now."

Ginger grimaced but removed her apron. "I hate to leave you with so many dishes. I have time to set out some more petit fours."

"Don't be silly. You've been a huge help all night, and while you're ovulating, no less."

They laughed, and Lisa hugged her. "Now, go. Babies are way more important than those women getting more cake."

"When you're right, you're right."

"I don't know about that, but I am the boss tonight."

With a wave, Ginger headed out the back door.

Lisa loaded a tray with petit fours, amazed at how many she'd already served. By the look of the leftovers, the guests had bypassed most of the candies she'd slaved over, but had taken to the cookies and the petit fours, small bites of cake, which she'd iced and decorated with individual rosebuds. Decorating cookies required a lot more work, as well as the initial cutting out and baking, but maybe she ought to consider cookie bouquets for her slow periods. College parents at the Kansas City universities might go for small care packages, especially around the holidays or exam time.

"I thought I'd find you in here."

Lisa dropped a petit four on another, smashing an iced flower. She ground her teeth then fixed a smile in place before facing Joe. Might as well start rehearsing now. She needed all the practice she could get pretending affection for someone putting her through such turmoil.

Of course he looked gorgeous, which should have helped the pretense but only made her more miserable. Why did he have to have the upper hand in everything? She felt as though she'd been working in a sweatshop all evening, while Joe looked sensational in a black suit, which made his black hair shine.

She bit back the temptation to tell him he looked handsome. Surely he heard that from women all the time, women who weren't pretending, women whose opinions mattered. She clamped her lips together.

"Are you hiding from my mother?"

"Absolutely."

His eyes widened, then he laughed. "For some reason, I thought you'd deny it."

She lifted a brow at him. "Some people enjoy honesty, Mr. Riley. Keeping track of lies is too exhausting."

His smile turned glacial. "Some people just can't loosen up. Anal, I believe Freud called it. Or just self-righteous."

Lisa flushed. When had she gotten to be such a sourpuss? Oh, yeah. Brad. She cleared her throat. "Sorry. I'm just nervous."

He looked genuinely surprised. "About meeting my mom? You shouldn't be. Mom's a sweetie pie."

She crossed her arms. "Then what was all that about our practicing kissing so she wouldn't see through our act? A bloodhound, I think you called her."

Joe grinned, showing his dimples. "I'm glad you reminded me. That's still a great idea."

"Forget it, buster." Lisa fought a giggle and lost. "You're looking for practice in all the wrong places."

"Nerves are making you hysterical. Let's go meet Mom and Dad and get this over with."

Her feet stuck to the floor. "Mom *and* Dad?"

"Sure, didn't I tell you? Mom's president of the Garden Society. Next to the Rose Exhibit, this is her big event. Naturally Dad came to support her."

"No," she said, her voice squeezing out of her tight throat. She pressed a hand to her abdomen. "You didn't mention it."

"Didn't Mom contact you about catering tonight?"

She rubbed her throbbing temple. "I dealt with the event coordinator, Lainey Perkins. I didn't know your mom was president."

He frowned. "It doesn't matter, does it?"

"I guess not. I just got this sick feeling in my stomach when you told me." She tried to laugh it off. "What difference could it possibly make?"

"Atta girl." Joe put his hand on the small of her back. He imagined her slender body perfectly curled into his. Her shiny blond hair would tickle like corn silk against his cheek. He enjoyed the warmth beneath his hand. Her derriere curved out right below. He could slide his hand down and—

And Lisa would smash an entire tray of desserts in his face. Joe smiled as he led her across the room. He enjoyed the fire of her temper, the challenge in her blue eyes. She didn't make it easy for him to "court" her, but he relished the chase. "There they are."

Lisa stumbled. He felt her stiffen as they neared and draped his arm across her back.

He tried to see them as Lisa would, but to Joe, they were just Mom and Dad. Joe inspected his mother's face for too much or too little color, but she appeared hale and hearty, despite the pressures of the evening. He let out a relieved breath. His dad beamed with pride, as if Mom had not only put this shindig together single-handedly but grown all the flowers, too. Joe felt that same satisfaction.

His mother watched their approach. He raised his voice to get his father's attention. "Mom, Dad. This is Lisa Meyer. Lisa, these are my parents, Alice and Mike Riley."

His dad encompassed her small hand with both of his. The warm, open smile on his face said better than his words how much he enjoyed meeting her. Lisa had helped make the party a success for his wife, and she was with Joe. That made her okay with his dad.

Joe glanced at his mom. She was sizing Lisa up, he noticed with fond amusement.

"So nice to meet you." His mom held out her hand to Lisa. "I've heard nothing but praise around the tables this evening, both for the taste of the desserts and for your smooth expertise in serving."

"Thank you." Lisa swallowed visibly. "It's nice of you to say so. I've enjoyed what I've seen of the flower exhibit. You've presented the flowers in a thought-provoking manner."

His mom's eyes narrowed. "How do you mean?"

Joe squeezed Lisa's waist.

She cleared her throat. "There are various ways to group a presentation. For instance, you could have put all the roses together, bunched the orchids, like that, displaying the quality of each entry against its rivals. But then you would have had a rose corner, an orchid corner, and so on, and it would have been boring, like picking out plants in a nursery."

Joe gawked at her. *Boring?* What was she doing? Why didn't she just say thanks to his mother's compliment, tell her how in love she was with him, and skedaddle back to the kitchen?

"I've seen it done totally by color, too."

He fought the urge to elbow her, fearing his mother would notice. With dread, he waited to hear what she'd say next because, as far as he could tell, his mom had grouped the flowers by color.

"That approach results in chaos, of course," Lisa said.

He groaned. Maybe she was showing her worst side, hoping his mother would talk Joe out of seeing her, declaring Lisa unfit. Or just insane.

"Chaos?" His mother's chill tone brought autumn to the room. He glanced at the nearby plants, watching for them to wither.

Lisa nodded. "Absolutely. Orchids and roses fighting for space, mixing their perfumes until it smelled like a funeral parlor—"

He choked, barely hearing his mother's gasp over the piano music in the background. His dad surveyed the nearby food tables, clearly not interested in flower arrangements and oblivious to the byplay.

"And obscuring their individual perfection. But—" Lisa's voice rose with what Joe took for enthusiasm "—you've utilized the color scheme, while preserving the distinctiveness of each species. Tea roses and old-fashioneds complement each other, and separating them by shade only emphasizes their individual characters."

Joe debated kicking her ankle. Had Lisa lost her mind? It hardly mattered that his mother was warming to her continued—and continued and continued—praise. He had to get her away. He observed her pinkened cheeks and bright eyes and finally noticed what had escaped him before.

Lisa wasn't breathing.

She'd barely taken a breath since she started. In a minute he'd have to scoop her off the floor from a light-headed faint. He no longer wanted to kick her ankle, although he might have to pound her on the back to get her to inhale. The tightness in his chest eased. She was only nervous, not trying to sabotage his plan.

"Well," he cut in, "we all agree with you, honey." He saw her start of surprise, and—finally, thankfully—heard her gulp in air. "When Mom does something, she does it right."

"That's what I was trying to say," Lisa said.

"I think I prefer her way of saying it," his mother said. "Much more effusive."

They all laughed.

"That's my girl." He leaned in to kiss Lisa's cheek.

She jumped back with wide eyes. His mother's mouth pursed. Slowly her narrowed gaze moved to Joe, connecting with his and sending a message.

Joe read her doubt all too clearly.

Lisa put her hand on his chest and peeked up at him. "I'm sorry. I'm just so jittery." She glanced at his parents, focusing on his dad. "I babble when I'm nervous, as you now know. Catering this event is so important to my business. I get dizzy thinking of the potential jobs I could book from all these people."

"Not to mention meeting us," his dad said. His friendliness relieved the tension among their group.

Lisa giggled. "Well, I wasn't going to mention that, but it is pretty scary, trying to win the parents' approval at the same time as the rest of this." She squinted toward Joe's mother. "No wonder I have a migraine."

"Oh, you poor dear." His mother tapped his dad's arm. "Go get my purse."

She turned back to Lisa as he left. "I have something that works wonders. I don't usually approve of taking medications, but look who I have to put up with."

"Humph." Joe acted offended, but he felt relieved. They'd discovered common ground, even if it was a headache. A woman approached his mom, who stepped away to listen to the lady's deafening praise for the event.

Lisa pivoted toward him and whispered, "I should have taken you up on your offer."

He frowned. His offer? "You already have my company's catering job. I'm really impressed with your work here tonight."

"No, your other offer." She leaned closer. "The kiss."

He blinked, then laughed as her color heightened. "It's not too late." He slid his arm down to her waist again and reeled her in flush against his body.

"Joe," Lisa hissed with a look over her shoulder at his mom. "We can't kiss here, in front of everybody."

"Sure we can. What would be more convincing?"

She tried to wriggle free.

"Oooh, keep it up. I like it."

She jabbed his ribs with her fist. He laughed and let her scoot back an inch.

"I have to go," his mother said, eyeing them. "Duty calls. It was lovely meeting you."

"And you," Lisa returned faintly. As soon as his mother moved out of earshot, she groaned. "That was awful."

He looked down at her in surprise. "I thought it went

pretty well." He laughed at her expression. "After you stopped talking, anyway."

"I think she saw us, you know, just now."

"Yeah." He frowned and rubbed his side. "Poking me won't make a very good impression."

She glared. "I meant that 'oooh, keep it up' nonsense."

"Lighten up. I doubt my mother thinks I'm a virgin."

Lisa glanced around frantically. "Would you please lower your voice? You might have told her I have kids, but she doesn't know whether I'm—" she moved close to whisper against his ear "—sexually active."

"Are you?" This sounded promising. And as oddly unsettling as her breath against his neck. He didn't like to think of her having sex with her dates, but he'd like to benefit from it if she did. The curious contradiction of his feelings bewildered him.

"Joe." She rubbed her temple. "You're exasperating."

"You can point out my personality flaws later. While we're practicing that kiss."

"I have work to do." She turned toward a serving table.

He followed. "When you're done, I'll take you home."

"I brought my own car, remember?"

"Lisa." He stopped her retreat by clasping her arm. "You know it's a good idea. Consider what a fiasco tonight could have been, with you jumping away from me." Remorse flashed in her eyes. With a little persuasion, he'd taste her sweetness by midnight. He should feel guilty, but healthy male interest squashed any chance of that. "I'll help you do dishes."

Lisa's mouth turned up in a reluctant smile. She glanced toward the loaded dessert table. "I accept."

The shrill tapping of silverware on glass made them turn.

"Ladies and gentlemen, your attention please." A dark-haired woman in a long, glittering aqua dress smiled from behind a microphone, setting aside the fork and goblet she'd used to gain notice. A small presentation area had been set up on a wooden stage two feet above the main floor. As the chatter died down, she continued, "I think we can all agree that tonight has been a tremendous success."

Joe and Lisa joined in the applause.

"So without further ado, let me introduce the woman responsible for our having such a wonderful year, President of the Howard Garden Society, Alice Riley."

Joe put two fingers to his mouth and whistled. Lisa's eyes fixed on his mother.

"Thank you," his mom said to the crowd. "As Lainey noted, it's been an exciting evening. We'll present the awards in a moment, but first I want to thank the people responsible for this success tonight. I especially want to thank Lainey Perkins and her committee for putting together a gala event."

Joe split his attention between Lisa and his mother as the committee members were named and the attendees clapped politely. Lisa had turned waxier than the gardenias.

"I'm so glad Lainey and her crew acquired the services of Goodies to Go. Lisa Meyer, the owner, outdid herself with those wonderful creations." His mom gestured toward Lisa.

Lisa flinched as everyone in the room looked at her, then she smiled at the applause.

When attention shifted back to his mother, Lisa leaned close and whispered, "Mentioning my business was sweet. I'll probably get a lot more calls now than just setting out my business cards produced." She sighed. "Maybe I was wrong."

"About what?"

"When she got up there, my stomach cramped again, like

in the kitchen." She shook her head. "I don't know why. That was a nice gesture."

"Another reason it's been such a great year for me," his mom continued, "is the return of my son to Howard."

Lisa stepped away as people turned to smile at him.

"Joe and his partner moved their company, Riley and Ross Electronics, here just ten months ago. Since Dylan Ross grew up here, many of you may remember him or know his mother, Betty, but Joe's new to Howard. So please welcome him to town before you leave this evening."

He smiled at his mom, dipping his head in thanks for the plug. Her returning smile showed more teeth than he would have liked. He caught Lisa's case of nerves as his mother leaned toward the microphone once more, eyes locked on his. He'd seen that intense look whenever she persuaded his dad to do something he didn't want to, like take time off work for a vacation or repaint the house. Joe swallowed. This wouldn't be good.

"While you're complimenting Lisa Meyer on her delicious treats, be sure to congratulate her, too," his mom continued without looking away from him. "She's just caught the most eligible bachelor in town. My son, Joe."

Chapter Four

"I'm sorry, I'm sorry," the rat said.

Lisa trudged passed Joe up her driveway, ignoring his presence. She wanted to scream with humiliation—at him, at his mother, at the moon. The night had been going so well, then bam! Alice Riley had taken Lisa's hard-won achievement and made it sound like a sordid favor. Shifting the box in her arms, Lisa dug for the house key in her slacks.

Joe appeared in her peripheral vision. "Let me help."

She glared at him, unsure whether he meant to put his hand in her pocket. It was unfair to punish the son for his mother's misdeeds, but Lisa didn't feel like being fair right then. She shoved the box so hard into his stomach his breath whooshed out. Grabbing the key, she thrust it into the lock and bumped open the door. At the last second, she remembered the kids—hopefully sleeping—and caught the door before it slammed against the wall. He followed her inside.

"Kitchen." She forced the word through gritted teeth. With more patience than she thought she possessed, she paid the babysitter and listened to her report on the kids. She stepped outside with Moneesha, trying to hurry the teen on her way. Lisa waited as the car started. Joe appeared at her side again, and her skin prickled. Hives, she thought. No doubt by tomorrow she'd be broken out in scaly blotches.

"As long as you're out here," she said through the smile she'd affected for Moneesha, "you can empty out the car."

"I'd be glad to. Then we have to talk."

"No." She waved to the girl's taillights and returned to the house. "We don't."

For the next few minutes, Joe followed her like a puppy, always underfoot, trying to please her. If he peed on the carpet, she'd do more than bat his nose with a newspaper.

When he set the last box on the kitchen counter, she forced herself to remember her manners. "Thanks for the help."

"You're welcome."

"Go home."

Joe just smiled at her.

"I don't think you heard me."

"You're awfully cute when you're mad."

Now he'd done it. The human male equivalent of peeing on the carpet. She lost hold of her frayed control and stalked toward him like a cat with a cornered mouse. "What did you say?"

He smiled wider. "You're cute when you're mad."

Lisa took a deep breath. He was baiting her, trying to get her to have it out with him. It wouldn't work. She smiled with false sweetness. "You're not being very cute right now. Why don't you go away and try again later?" She snapped her fingers, as though an idea had just occurred to her. "Better yet, why don't you just go away?"

"You're starting to like me. I can tell."

Lisa glanced around the room, searching for a newspaper to roll up. Or a tire iron. Not seeing either one handy, she glared at Joe. "This isn't going to work between us. Forget the catering contract. Forget the whole thing."

"But it *is* working. My mom's thrilled."

She growled at him and headed toward the front room. Tonight had been a roller coaster of emotions. She'd ridden to a successful business high only to fall with acute personal embarrassment. The adventure made her stomach hurt. "It's working for you, maybe."

"Better than I'd planned." He grinned. "I never would have imagined Mom would like you so much she'd announce our engagement to all her friends."

Lisa's mouth opened, but she couldn't find any words. She was mortified—and amazed that Joe didn't get it. This was a disaster. She dropped onto the sofa, propped her elbows on her knees and leaned her head in her hands. She wouldn't cry. No matter how awful the night had been, she promised herself she wouldn't cry. Not until he left, anyway.

"What's the problem?" He moved around behind the couch and placed his hands on her shoulders. "Mom and Dad both liked you." He began to knead her muscles. "That was the idea, right?"

"Right." Her voice came out muffled, but she didn't want to raise her head. His fingers worked magic, smoothing out tense knots, easing away her headache. She decided to let him stay a few more minutes.

"Everything's on schedule." His thumbs stroked up the furrows beside her vertebrae, digging in enough to please without pinching or pressing too hard. She bit back a moan.

"The hardest part is done," he said. "We see my folks a few times, then presto." He sat beside her and slid a hand up to massage her neck. "You're off the hook."

"But…" She looked at Joe, feeling off center. His soothing tone and wonderful massage evaporated her anger, leaving only confusion. "We're engaged."

"Nah. Mom likes to be in charge, but I still do my own proposing." He grinned, and this time it reassured rather than annoyed her. "Don't worry. I won't let my mother trick you into actually walking down the aisle."

Lisa smiled in return, too tired to fight anymore. The entire day had wreaked havoc with her nerves. She'd never catered a party that large, and the responsibility had made her jittery. The added strain of impressing the guests so they'd consider her for future catering jobs, combined with meeting Joe's parents, had made her feel like a lame cat in a room full of coyotes.

"None of those women will take me seriously now. They'll think I got the Garden Society job because of you, not because of my catering skills."

Joe put his arm around her shoulder and squeezed, shaking his head. "They tasted your goodies, Lisa. They won't care whether I have or not."

She elbowed him in the ribs.

He laughed. "Your service is impeccable. The trays stayed filled, the dirty dishes disappeared, and your sweet offerings—what I've sampled, anyway—were delicious and presented artistically. Agreeable to the eye, but not so fancy anyone would hesitate to eat them."

Lisa blinked, surprised and pleased he'd noticed those details. He'd assessed her work as a future client. She'd forgotten she was auditioning her business for him, as well. Out of gratitude for his much-needed praise, she ignored the crack about sampling her sweet offerings. "Thanks. You can be very thoughtful."

"I have my moments."

"I guess you do."

"Now, about that kiss." His smirk challenged her to keep her temper.

What harm could come from a few kisses? It wasn't as though she'd fall for the guy, fully aware of his tendency to alter the truth to suit his needs.

She accepted his unspoken challenge, but on her own terms. Leaning toward him, she cupped the back of his head. Before he could draw breath, Lisa kissed him. She drew back and studied his flabbergasted expression with triumph. "You're not much of a kisser."

Joe's mouth opened and closed like a trout on a riverbank.

"Maybe we ought to rehearse," she taunted, using his own words against him from when she'd accepted the bargain in his office. She'd have to pay later for tormenting him, but she enjoyed having the upper hand at the moment. She leaned in and rubbed her lips across his, stopping to suck his lower lip. With a gentle nip, she released him. "That's probably enough for now. I don't want to overwhelm you."

She chuckled as he straightened. His hands tightened on her upper arms, stalling her backward motion. She grinned, savoring the game. She hadn't flirted in years. She'd married What's-his-name right out of high school, being slightly pregnant, and certainly hadn't dated since he left. Maybe she wasn't dead at twenty-six, after all.

Joe flexed his hands, tempted to kiss the socks off her—and a few other garments while he was at it. When she closed her eyes and parted her lips, the urge to crush her against him clutched at his gut. He could feel her warm breath on his cheek. Every cell—especially every hormone—screamed for him to take her up on her offer.

And, brother, had she offered. She'd as good as dared

him. Joe fought against picking up the gauntlet she'd tossed and sliding it into her until they both shrieked with pleasure.

As if she'd appreciate that idea. He grunted.

"Hmm?" Lisa murmured, eyes still closed, waiting for his kiss.

He leaned closer. His lips brushed her cheek. "We need to talk."

"Talk?" Lisa blinked, looking adorably dazed and malleable.

That ought to teach her to tease him. He lounged back against the sofa and savored the sensation of having Lisa off-kilter, but tried not to look smug. "How did we meet?"

She blinked again. "How did we...?" She took a breath, then scowled. "You came to my house to manipulate me in to—"

Joe shook his head, hiding his irritation behind a tolerant smile. "You can't tell people that, especially not my mother."

"Oh." She cleared her throat. "Well, I wouldn't say it in quite that way to her."

"Good thing," he muttered, "since I did not manipulate you."

"You tried."

He raised a brow at her, attempting to appear reasonable. "As I remember it, you came to my office, promising me anything, if only I'd help you."

"The way you *choose* to remember it," Lisa said, "isn't anything we could tell people, either."

He nodded. "So how do you want us to meet?"

She wedged herself into the corner of the couch, half facing him, while increasing the distance between them. He'd bet his next contract she'd done it intentionally.

"We're making up our meeting?" she asked.

"Our whole relationship. It's all a pretense," he said, overriding what looked to be another objection from her. "We'd better have matching stories."

She grimaced. "I see your point, but I still don't like lying."

"'Oh, what a tangled web we weave' and all that?"

"Mock me if you will, but I'm basically an honest person. I'm trying to set a good example for my kids." She frowned. "After all the deception they've had to deal with from their father, they deserve someone they can believe in."

What had he stepped in the middle of? A deceptive father. An uptight mom. Sheesh. All he needed was a fake fiancée. He adjusted his position on the couch, more uncomfortable with his part in this than he wanted to admit. It was supposed to be a harmless lark, just a smoke screen to put his mother off the scent until she recovered her full health.

He ought to opt out now before anyone got hurt. He'd never dated a woman with children. He didn't want to make Lisa's kids think of her as a liar. This was getting messy.

On the other hand, maybe he could do some good here. Winning over the kids would be a good way to thank Lisa for her help. He'd show them not all men were jerks. When they let go of their hostility, she'd probably be so relieved she'd fall into his arms. He welcomed the idea. His recent dry spell since moving to Howard made him antsy. The time had come to indulge in some fun.

And he knew just the woman he wanted to indulge with. He watched her nibble her lush bottom lip, thinking he'd like to nibble on her. It wasn't as though he'd fall for her, what with her uptight ways. But oh, he thought, eyes on her glistening mouth. How he'd love to help her have some fun, preferably in bed with him.

"How about this? I met your kids at a field trip to our

firm—" He stopped when Lisa shook her head. He agreed. Too convoluted. "Okay, I spoke at their school, and they came up afterw—" He scowled. Her danged head would fall off if she didn't quit shaking it. "What's the matter?"

"We're not involving my children. Remember, that was my condition for agreeing."

"I agreed to act—honorably, I believe was your word—when I was around them."

"They're not to be dragged into your schemes."

"Yeah, but it's not as bad as all—"

"Not bad? Your mother announced our engagement tonight."

"See?" He grinned. "The kids are practically family."

She rolled her eyes. "No."

Joe snorted. He definitely had to work on her fun threshold. "Don't worry. We'll come up with something."

Lisa crossed her arms over her chest. A sure sign of stress. "You're persistent, but you don't listen."

"I listen. I'm just not following your orders."

"I'm the mom."

Joe hooted. "Not mine."

The glint in her eyes hardened. "I'm the mom in this house. You want to be invited to this house, you follow my rules."

He couldn't resist. He cupped the back of her head and kissed her breathless, then gazed into her stunned face. "We'll work it out."

"I'm not something you need to work out," she said, making him wish he hadn't backed off. It just gave her the opportunity to argue. "My kids don't even like you."

Joe smiled, identifying Step One. He studied what he could see of the house while they concocted the story of their relationship. Her kids didn't like him? That, he could fix.

THOSE DARNED KIDS just didn't like him.

They weren't even trying. Since he'd gone out and bought them a video game system with all the newest game cartridges, he'd thought they'd warm up a little. He didn't expect them to fall at his feet, but a show of gratitude wouldn't hurt.

Of course, they no doubt learned ingratitude from their mother. She'd clamped her lips together the minute she opened the door to him, while he stood on the porch like a springtime Santa Claus, his arms full of gifts and feeling pretty proud of himself. It didn't appear she'd be able to open her mouth for a long time. Not that he wanted her to. The murder scheme in her eyes expressed her feelings clearly enough.

Stubborn female.

He laid out his gifts on the coffee table while the three watched. His back prickled as the silence grew. When he straightened, he saw the kids huddled by the doorway and Lisa only steps inside the room, halfway between. As though the kids needed protecting from him. His jaw tightened.

Abby and Bobby threw him sidelong glances and muttered under their breath, no doubt hatching some plot to poison him. He was the enemy. The dreaded gift-giver.

Sheesh. Even the kids needed to lighten up.

The children turned as one and stood with their hands behind their backs, looking innocent. Joe tensed against their attack.

"We're sorry," said Abby, as spokesperson. "We can't accept your…presents."

He didn't care for her pause. Gesturing toward the boxes, he said, "I can exchange it for something you'd like better, if you already have this game system."

The longing in their eyes gave them away. They wanted it bad. The clamp on Bobby's jaw spoke for them, too. They had no intention of accepting. Not from him, anyway. This second meeting with the kids wasn't going much better than when they'd first seen him arguing with their mother. At least he wasn't hobbled with pain this time.

"Thank you, but no," Abby said.

Where did an eight-year-old learn such self-possession? Oh, yeah. Joe darted a glance at Lisa. Ms. Rigid.

"My dad will get this for us when he comes home," Bobby said, his chest thrust out. "We don't need you to buy us anything."

"Bobby, that's not polite," Lisa said. Her eyes had filled with tears.

"You're being stupid, too," Abby added. She shoved his shoulder. "Dad's not coming back. Ever."

"Abby, don't call your bro—" Lisa started.

"He doesn't want to be our dad anymore," the girl finished.

Lisa made a choking sound.

Abby continued. "It's never gonna be like before. Dad divorced us. He's not going to come back and live with us."

"Abby, your dad didn't divorce you and Bobby," Lisa said.

The children turned to face her. She crossed the room to stand before them. Joe figured he might as well be invisible, and he pretty much wished he were. It seemed this would become an intense family discussion, which made him itchy. He slouched on the couch, forgotten in the midst of more important issues, wishing he'd brought his laptop. With a sigh, he remembered his PDA and took it out.

Lisa took a breath and forced herself to meet their gazes without flinching. She hoped the right words would come. "Your dad didn't want to leave you. He only divorced me, but he couldn't stay here with you after that." She lowered her voice, ready to lie for her kids, but not wanting Joe to hear her. Although he seemed to have lost interest in the conversation. "That doesn't mean he doesn't think about you every day and want you to be together."

Abby's too-old eyes broke her heart with their doubt.

Bobby's innocent gaze appeared hopeful but hesitant. "Do you think so? Dad wants to be part of our family again?"

Lisa groped for words. "Your dad is a part of your family, and he always will be. It's just…" She spread her hands. The gesture must look as lost as she felt. "He and I aren't family anymore. We share you two, and we share memories of the life we had."

Some of which she'd rather not keep, like Brad running off with the then twenty-year-old Lacey, a bouncy blonde bimbette, who popped her gum, for heaven's sakes, and wore skimpy blouses, showing off her flat midriff. And the ring in her pierced belly button. Having seen her at Brad's office on the rare occasion she'd visited, Lisa would never have thought Lacey the type to catch his eye. Although, perhaps it wasn't his eye she'd caught.

But as Lisa gazed at her two beautiful children, she knew she'd be eternally grateful Brad had given her these precious gifts. "We share a bond, your father and I. We share you two. We're both your parents, no matter where we are."

Or how we act, she thought with a touch of acid.

"But," she added aloud, "he won't be coming back to live with us. Understand?"

Abby nodded but studied the carpet. Lisa couldn't tell how her daughter felt.

"Abby, don't you have something to say to your brother?"

"Sorry I called you stupid."

"'S okay." Bobby scowled and pointed behind Lisa. "What about him?"

It took her a second to remember Joe. She glanced over her shoulder at him, resting comfortably while she struggled with allaying her children's feelings of parental abandonment.

Sure, he could lounge. He had no responsibilities. He had no major debt trying to drag him under. As a hotshot electronics guru in his early thirties, he probably had a bank balance in the bazillions. "What about him?"

"Didn't he try to bribe us?" Bobby clarified.

In her attempt to reassure them of their father's love, she'd forgotten how all this started. It was Joe's fault, and she'd be darned if she'd let him off the hook so easily. She'd learned that lesson in her marriage. Let the guy squirm on the line for once. Granted, Joe wasn't their father, but why should she have to explain his actions?

"It's rude to speak in front of someone as if they aren't in the room. If you have a question for Mr. Riley, ask him." She gave Joe a beatific smile.

The glimmer in his eyes acknowledged her tactic. He tipped his head to her. Appreciation for her cleverness or a promise of retaliation later?

"Well?" Bobby asked in a belligerent tone.

Both children waited for his answer with narrowed eyes. The jury had decided before the defendant even testified. Lisa bit her bottom lip. Maybe she should bail Joe out—not for his sake, she denied quickly to the feminist voice in her head that chided her for a wimp, but for the kids.

Before she finished her inner battle, he spoke.

"It looks that way, I know. I didn't mean to do anything to hurt your feelings, but I can't deny I hoped to win some points."

Three people gaped at him.

He shrugged. "It's the truth, and you know how big your mom is on honesty." He smiled, and Lisa wondered if he'd heard her sidestepping the truth earlier.

"I noticed you didn't have a game system," he said, "so I thought you might like me more if I gave you one, and before I could think better of it, here I am." He spread his hands, echoing Lisa's earlier gesture.

Lisa crumpled inside. A man admitting his mistake. She didn't know what effect his confession had on the kids, but she definitely liked him better. She swiveled to face the children.

They looked confused, and she couldn't blame them. What would they think of Joe now? Yes, he'd tried to buy their affections, but he realized he'd done wrong, and admitted it. That must blow them away. Even though she'd always acknowledged her mistakes, Brad had believed it would diminish his authority. He'd set himself up as infallible. When he'd walked out, the kids assumed he'd been right to do so. Lisa had spent the past eighteen months helping them see otherwise.

"What do you think?" she asked the kids, holding her breath. Rooting for Joe, she realized. Who'd have thought it?

"He tried to buy us," Bobby said.

"As if," Abby snubbed Joe.

Lisa scowled at Abby's rudeness and Bobby's rigidity. "Okay, you're right. He shouldn't have done it."

They nodded.

"But," she continued, "it's kind of a compliment."

They stared as though she'd grown another head.

"Don't you think it's sort of nice Mr. Riley thinks so much of you he'd want you to like him?"

"Yeah, I guess so." Bobby scuffed his toe in the carpet. "I didn't think of it like that."

Abby snorted. "He wants us to like him because he likes you, Mom. He doesn't really care about us."

Lisa turned to Joe. She wanted to reassure Abby, but that wouldn't be fair to any of them. "Joe?"

He rose and smiled at her daughter. "You're half-right, Abby, just like kids usually are."

Lisa rolled her eyes. The idiot was going to patronize them.

"You can see only part of the picture," he continued, "because you've lived part of your life. When you're—"

Please don't say *older,* Lisa begged silently.

"—more experienced—"

She blew out her breath.

"—you'll be able to understand more things. I like your mom. We have…a business deal to conduct, and I'd like to take her out occasionally. It'd make things easier for me if you liked me, and that's partly why I brought you guys a present."

Abby folded her arms over her chest and waited. Bobby scowled.

"What you don't see yet is that I picked a present I thought you'd both like, something I cared enough to notice you didn't have. Hopefully, I got games a boy or a girl would enjoy."

"But you did it to impress Mom," Abby said.

Joe smirked. "Does your mom look impressed?"

The kids smiled. Lisa fought to keep her expression stern.

"It didn't work out the way you planned," Abby countered, "but you still wanted to get to Mom through us."

Joe shook his head.

"You said—"

"I said I wanted you guys to like me better. I said it would make it easier for me to come around. But I know your mother won't like me just because you do." He winked at the kids. "I'm still thinking of a present to buy her affections."

Lisa tried to appear outraged at the idea she could be bought, but Joe mocking himself was irresistible. Abby must have thought so, too, because she laughed with him.

Bobby glared. "Are we still mad at him or what?"

The room fell silent.

"Nah. Just don't do it again," Abby warned Joe. "We're not easy to buy off."

Joe nodded. He and Abby shared a smile of understanding, which amazed Lisa. Maybe having Joe around her children wasn't such a bad thing after all.

"So," Bobby said, "if we're not mad, do we get to keep the bribe?"

"No." Abby patted her brother's drooping shoulders. "It wouldn't be right. But we can like him now."

"Oh." Bobby dragged himself out of the room with Abby behind him, offering to let him pick a DVD movie to watch together.

"I don't care if they keep it," Joe said.

Lisa shook her head. "You didn't mean any harm, but it wouldn't be right to accept an expensive gift from you."

He stared at her with an incredulous expression. "What decade are you from?"

She shrugged, not taking offense. "We don't have much, but we have our pride."

"I'll say," he muttered.

"Thanks for telling the kids the truth about your intentions. It meant a lot to me."

Ruefully, he shook his head. "This family is so weird. You want the damn present, but you won't keep it. However, you will forgive me for giving it to you."

She laughed. "I didn't say I'd forgiven you."

But she had. His hangdog expression, although feigned,

looked so adorably repentant she couldn't stay mad. She knew he'd learned from his mistake. What mother wouldn't be touched by a man who tried to get her kids to like him?

She invited Joe to stay for dinner and enjoyed watching him with the kids, who had to explain most of the phrases they used and all of the music they talked about. Abby wisely didn't mention Juniper Jones. Spaghetti, a meal Lisa could serve him without killing her budget, had never tasted so satisfying. Her warm feelings toward Joe lasted for the rest of the evening.

Right up until he got in his car, lowered his window and spoke. "My parents invited you to dinner. I said Friday would be fine."

Chapter Five

Lisa swallowed hard as Joe stopped his small sports car in front of his parents' Cape Cod–style home on Friday night. Tall old oak trees waved their newly leafed branches above, while fresh green lawns sparkled at their bases. Despite the peace of the surroundings, Lisa dreaded the evening ahead.

"Why are you glaring at me?" Joe asked.

She started. "I didn't realize I had been."

"That's not likely to convince my parents you're madly in love with me or that we want to spend the rest of our lives together."

"Sorry. I won't glare at you when they're watching."

Joe gave her an ironic look. "Gee, thanks."

Lisa doubted she could deceive the Rileys all night without confessing. She could imagine their sense of betrayal if she blurted out the truth. *I'm not in love with your son. I barely like him, and I'm sure not marrying him.*

She glanced at Joe and wondered at the truth of her statement. Not the part about marrying him—she'd never get married again. But did she like him? He certainly attracted her. She'd found him physically appealing right from the start, when she'd thought him a salesman come to tempt her.

Well, she was tempted. His kisses the other evening had reawakened some long-dead parts of her, and not just physical places, either.

But *like* him?

He came around and opened her door, and Lisa forced herself out of the car. She wanted to linger, not only to avoid his parents, but because the sports car's leather seats and luxurious appointments made her feel pampered. Something she never felt in her nine-year-old clunker.

"Ready?" he asked.

No, she thought, but nodded and brushed at the skirt of her turquoise cotton dress to loosen any wrinkles. She passed tulips of every hue, white hyacinths and some other small flowers she thought grew from bulbs. They enveloped her in their thick scent. If she suffered from allergies, she could have gotten watery eyes and sinus blockage and excused herself early. But darn her luck, she could breathe just fine.

"Lisa, come in, come in," Alice said, hand outstretched. Mike smiled a welcome. If only they'd been hostile, Lisa thought wistfully. Things just weren't going her way.

Alice's petite stature next to her tall, lumberjack-built husband only made her appear more delicate. Her soft white curls reminded Lisa of marshmallows, but her diamond-blue eyes watched every move Lisa made, especially as Joe took her wrap and led her into the dining room. She sighed as she passed homey stitcheries and collectible knickknacks. The maple table gleamed with polish, and the food smelled heavenly. A home-cooked meal Lisa hadn't had to prepare was an undeserved pleasure. She sat across from Alice, feeling like Judas at the Last Supper.

"I wish you'd brought the children," Alice said while serving the entrée. "We'd so like to meet them."

Lisa stiffened, unsure what to say. The chicken and rice on her plate congealed before her eyes. The heavy white sauce on the asparagus made her stomach churn but provided her with inspiration. "They're not very good eaters."

"We could work around that," Mike said on her right side at the head of the table. So eager, so accommodating, so darn nice. "Maybe we could go on a picnic. Kids still like hot dogs and chips, right? We could go someplace they could run around, play ball."

The elder Rileys gazed at her with hope lighting their faces. Hating to disappoint them, Lisa reconsidered. Would it really be so bad to have a picnic together? A simple meal in the sunshine?

No, no, no. She couldn't drag the children into this farce. She didn't need more complications. But Alice and Mike just looked at her, and she floundered. Why didn't Joe help her out? Joe, with his charming manner and smooth tongue, sat silently watching. The skunk.

How could she refuse? She couldn't, not outright, not without breaking her agreement with Joe. She'd have to stall. "Maybe we can do that sometime."

"I'll check the weather report tonight," Mike said.

"Well," Lisa hedged, "the kids still have school. Homework. Sports events. It might not be right away."

"Then I'll check *The Old Farmer's Almanac* for June."

She shifted in her chair and looked to change the subject, unaccustomed to lying, and disliking Silent Joe more by the moment. But you agreed, a shrill voice needled her. You got yourself into this mess.

Lisa turned to her hostess. "Mrs. Riley, this chicken smells delicious. What did you use for seasoning?"

Alice squinted at her across the table. "Thirty cloves of garlic."

Like thirty pieces of silver, Lisa's conscience poked her. She swallowed. "Oh. You'd think it'd be overwhelming, but it's not."

"It has to cook all day."

"Did you grow the garlic yourself?"

"I buy garlic at the grocery store." Alice's eyebrows rose. "I bought the chicken there, too."

Lisa felt like an idiot. The silence yawned wide as a chasm. Three pairs of eyes regarded her, as though her spaceship had just landed. "I thought maybe you grew herbs, since you're in the Garden Society."

Alice shook her head.

"Is garlic an herb," Lisa asked, needing to fill the silence, "or a spice? Or, well, maybe something else. Just a regular plant, like a vegetable?"

Alice frowned, but whether she wondered which family garlic belonged to or why her son had brought this nutcase to her house, she didn't say. Nobody said anything.

"Not that you have to grow things to eat. Flowers are nice, too." Lisa dug herself in deeper, a little desperate now, the silence cloaking her like wet wool. Had she insulted Alice's gardening by making flowers sound frivolous? "My mom grew flowers before she moved to Arizona. Now she grows cactus. Cacti."

She giggled, almost hysterical with nerves.

All three Rileys stared at her.

Then Joe smiled. "Mom's an award-winner, aren't you, Mom?"

Lisa's breath whooshed out, and she drooped in her chair.

Alice blushed. "Now, Joe."

"Go on, tell Lisa about your roses."

"That's just silly. She doesn't want to hear about my little hobby."

Lisa smiled in relief. "I'd love to hear about it." If someone else talked, she wouldn't start up again. Why did silence unnerve her so?

"It's more than a hobby, Mother," Mike declared. He leaned across the corner of the table toward Lisa. "Mother likes to pretend it's nothing, but let me tell you, she works hard for her awards. One year we won the Green Thumb Award for the Prettiest Yard in the City—"

"Mike, that's enough," Alice cut in.

"But do you know what?" he asked in a lowered voice.

Lisa shook her head, pulled in by his conspiratorial tone. She didn't want to take sides or upset Mrs. Riley, but Mike's good-spirited teasing intrigued her.

"Mike," Alice called his name in warning.

"She made me put *my* name on the entry form so she wouldn't get the attention."

Lisa grinned with the two men.

Alice's face turned red. "Michael Riley—"

"Stood over my shoulder and told me what to write."

"You're not supposed to tell anyone that!"

Joe laughed. "This is the first I've heard of it."

"They're not just anyone," Mike said. "They're family."

Lisa's breath caught. She wasn't family. She wouldn't ever be. She didn't deserve to know the Rileys' secrets.

"Well, then," Alice said, "I'll tell them how you spend all your time in your workshop. I'm not the only one with a hobby."

Mike's eyes gleamed. "Yes, but I don't win awards."

Alice slumped in her seat, her gaze on the embroidered tablecloth.

Lisa frowned in confusion. "But winning awards is something to be proud of, Mrs. Riley."

The older woman shook her head.

"Pride is a sin." Mike took his wife's hand. She raised her head and stared into his eyes. "And my little Alice is a sinner."

They shared a look so intimate Lisa had to glance away. Her gaze landed on Joe, whose mouth hung open. She nudged him with her foot.

Joe turned wide eyes toward her then snapped his mouth shut. She couldn't help but smile. He'd just been slapped in the face with an unpalatable truth. His parents had sex. Still. And apparently enjoyed it. His astonishment made her giggle.

"Of course, we've been *married* for forty years," his mother said in a tight tone.

Lisa glanced at her. Alice's rigid expression shouted disapproval. She'd obviously misinterpreted the laughter Lisa had shared with Joe.

"Save it for after the ceremony, son," Mike added.

Lisa's face heated. She didn't dare look at Joe.

"Speaking of which," Alice said, as casually as though discussing the latest Royals' baseball scores, passing the basket of dinner rolls to her husband, "when is the wedding?"

"I haven't actually proposed yet, Mom."

Alice waved away that insignificant detail. "You don't want to wait too long. Autumn flowers just don't decorate a church the way roses do."

"Thanks to nurseries, we can have any flower, whenever we want," he countered.

"What's your favorite flower?" Alice asked, eyes burning into Lisa's.

She searched her mind for something which didn't bloom anytime soon. "Poinsettias."

Alice beamed and slapped the table. "That's settled then. A Christmas wedding."

Joe cleared his throat. "Except that I haven't proposed, Mom, and Lisa hasn't accepted."

Alice turned to Lisa, her expression wounded. "Why don't you want to marry Joe?"

"I didn't say I wouldn't—" Lisa snapped her mouth shut. Alice's eyes glittered with triumph. Lisa didn't dare look at Joe. She'd very nearly accepted his mother's proposal. How humiliating.

"I'll keep that in mind," Joe said with a hint of humor.

His parents laughed, no doubt delighted. His comment only reinforced their belief in the pretense.

Lisa buried her face in her hands, tempted to excuse herself to use the powder room, but unsure what trouble Joe would get them into if she left the table. They'd probably have the church booked by the time she returned.

"Can't rush these things, though," Joe said.

"Well, why not?" Alice wanted to know. "You said you've been dating for a few months. You've obviously anticipated the wedding night, if those looks you keep giving Lisa are any indication."

"Mom!"

Lisa's head shot up. Joe was giving her looks? Their heated kiss after the Garden Society fiasco popped into her mind. She'd thought he'd only been teasing her. Was he attracted to her beyond their arrangement? Or was it all part of his act?

"We understand," Mike said, his tone placating. "But Mother and I don't feel you should be carrying on like this in front of Lisa's children."

"We're not," Lisa blurted out.

"Dad—"

"Well, now, maybe you're not doing anything *in front* of the children—"

"I should hope not," Alice muttered.

Oh, for heaven's sakes, Lisa thought, watching them "communicate." She felt as though she were driving by a roadside accident—appalled, but unable to look away. The elder Rileys didn't listen at all. They just assumed, then the conversation spun out of control.

"But that doesn't mean the kids don't know what's going on," Mike said.

"Nothing's going on," Joe replied with a clenched jaw. "What we do, or don't do, is none of your business."

"Of course it's our business," Alice insisted.

"They're going to be our grandchildren," Mike said.

"No, they're not." Lisa stood up and threw her cloth napkin beside her plate. It seemed the only way to get their attention. This had to stop. Poor Joe, being railroaded. Surely in all his years as their son, he'd learned how to talk to them? Of course, if he had, she wouldn't be in this predicament.

"Now, Lisa." Alice rose from her chair, then wobbled and sat abruptly. "Oh, my."

Mike raced to her side. "Honey?"

"Mom, are you okay?" Joe squatted beside her.

Each man held a hand, patting. Lisa wondered that neither checked Alice's pulse.

"I'm fine," she assured them in a quavering tone.

"Do you need your pills?" her husband asked.

Alice patted her forehead with her napkin. "No, dear, I'll be all right. I shouldn't have gotten so overwrought."

Lisa narrowed her eyes. Alice might appear flushed, but unnaturally so? The timing was more than convenient.

"Hand me my water please," Alice said to Joe, who rushed it to her.

Instead of sipping, she pressed the glass to her forehead, dampening her skin. Her eyelids fluttered.

"You should lie down," Mike said.

"No, I'm fine, or at least I will be in a moment."

"Dad's right." Joe rubbed her arm. "No sense overdoing it."

"But we have company."

Lisa softened her smile, though her suspicious mind remained hard at work. "I wouldn't dream of staying while you're ill."

For a moment, she imagined a flash of steel in the glare Alice shot her, but it vanished in an instant.

"Thank you for dinner," Lisa said. "I hope you're feeling better soon."

Joe rose and followed her from the room. He didn't say anything until he pulled into her driveway. Then it was a terse, "I'll call you."

She glanced at him, startled. Was he just worried about his mother's health or was he angry? She'd said her kids would never be the Rileys' grandchildren, but she hadn't meant to renege on her arrangement with Joe.

Lisa nodded and got out of the car. He pulled away the moment she closed the door, leaving her on the sidewalk, watching him drive away from her.

Oh, God, what had she done?

"It was terrible," Lisa told Ginger the next morning in her kitchen. Abby sat on the front porch with another girl from school, no doubt plotting how to get Lisa to change her mind regarding Sally Turner's party. Bobby had gone to soccer practice with Mark, a boy from his team.

Ginger patted her hand. "I'm sure it seemed so at the time."

"At the time?" Lisa rose from the kitchen chair and paced away. Wispy curtains let too much sunshine in through the windows. She pivoted away, the light hurting her tired eyes. She hadn't slept. Memories of the previous night had replayed in her mind like a DVD player gone haywire.

Alice's disapproving face. Mike's eagerness to meet the children. Their insistence on Joe marrying her soon. Their certainty she and Joe had anticipated their vows. Her own suspicions regarding Alice's health.

The leashed anger in Joe's voice as he'd spoken his last words to her.

She rubbed her temple. "It was a nightmare."

Ginger turned toward her. "So, they want you guys to get married. That's what prompted this whole thing in the first place. Why are you surprised?"

"I'm not." Lisa flopped back down on the chair. "I just hadn't expected them to be so pushy at our first dinner."

"If his mom wasn't pushy, Joe wouldn't be in this mess."

"I felt ambushed. They want so badly to meet Abby and Bobby. They almost started in on us having had sex already." She sipped some iced tea.

Ginger's eyebrows rose. "Why did they assume you'd had sex?"

"Something about the way Joe looks at me." Lisa darted a glance at Ginger. "I'm sure they're imagining things."

"Are you?"

Lisa stroked condensation off the glass, not meeting Ginger's gaze. "Well, sure. We aren't involved, not romantically. Just to deceive his parents."

"Maybe you should change the way you think about this."

"I have. I told them I wouldn't marry Joe. Well, I said Abby and Bobby wouldn't be their grandchildren, which is the same thing."

"Lisa, you didn't."

"Oh, yeah. I did. I guess I've lost his company's job now." She groaned. "He'll want the advance back."

"Slow down." Ginger put a hand on Lisa's forearm where it rested on the table. "I'm sure they realize you were distraught. You can still go through with the pretense."

"But I don't want to."

"Look, you weren't prepared last night. Just have Joe tell them you guys made up and everything's back on."

Lisa stared at her. "Why would I want to do that?"

"Do you have the advance money to return to Joe?"

"Most of it. I had to pay for Bobby's program."

"Most may not be good enough. You signed a contract to cater his party. If you renege, you're legally bound to return all the advance money."

Lisa sighed. "I can probably return the rest next month. I have two bookings coming up." She slid a glance at Ginger. "One's from someone who attended the Garden Society party. The Marshalls' daughter's baby shower. Ironic, huh?"

Ginger smiled. "It's your scrumptious desserts that got the bookings, hon, not your supposed relationship to the Rileys."

"Right. I'll try to think of it like that."

"You need to think of something else in a different light."

"What?"

"Joe."

Lisa blanked her expression—she hoped. "There's nothing to think about with Joe."

"I disagree. You refer to your agreement as deceiving Joe's parents. Why don't you view it as saving Joe? Or doing Joe a favor so he doesn't have to hurt his parents?"

"Because he *is* hurting them, Ginger. He's lying to them."

"It's not the best course, I agree. But you said he'd tried being straightforward, and his mom ignored him. Honesty didn't work. Short of cutting his parents out of his life, what else can he do? Let her ruin his business by sending women to his meetings?"

"I don't know." Lisa propped her elbows on the table and rested her chin on her palms.

"You've seen them in action firsthand," Ginger continued, on a mission now. "You know how relentless and overbearing they can be."

"Definitely."

"You know what Joe's been up against. Now add to that his love for his parents, and the poor guy's trapped in a corner."

Lisa took a breath, then, needing a sounding board, described Alice's conveniently timed "attack."

"Do you think she's faking it?" Ginger asked.

"It's a possibility. If we'd been discussing anything else, I'd probably think she got light-headed. Given the circumstances, though, I have to wonder."

"It'd be easier if you knew for sure, but either way, it's just another reason to side with Joe."

Lisa stared at Ginger. The sunlight behind her radiated through her apricot hair. A spark lit her green eyes. "You look like an avenging angel."

"I feel sorry for him. He's got impossible parents, a strong sense of love and duty, and his only ally retreated from the battlefield."

"It's not like that," Lisa said, slighted, but feeling guilty,

"It's exactly like that. So, you were uncomfortable with them wanting to meet the kids and pushing for a wedding date. Think how Joe's been feeling. He actually cares what they think, and he's worried about his mom's health."

"I care, too."

"Lisa, you're my best friend, so I'm going to be blunt. You care about your integrity, which is fine, but you put his parents' feelings before Joe's."

Lisa couldn't believe her friend didn't understand why his behavior upset her. How could she stand by Joe when it entailed deceit? "You're supposed to be on my side."

"I am. Always." Ginger squeezed Lisa's hand. "I'm saving you from doing something you'll regret later."

Lisa conceded the point, having already felt that stab of guilt. "This is a dilemma, Gin. I want to help him, but I don't approve of this deception."

"Can you blame him? Honesty failed, and you've seen how persistent they are. Which is the lesser evil? You lying to his parents or you backing out on your word?"

Lisa withstood her friend's forthright gaze. She didn't care for her own reflection as seen through those eyes. She sighed. "Sometimes I really hate you."

Ginger smiled and patted her wrist. "You're welcome."

Lisa wet her throat with some tea. They'd spent too long talking about her problems. "How's the Baby Project going?"

Ginger withdrew her hand, her expression now a blank.

"What's wrong?" Lisa asked.

"I'm not pregnant yet."

Lisa blinked. Her friend's flat tone turned the remark into self-recrimination. "I'm sorry, sweetie. But you and Kyle haven't been trying that long."

Ginger grimaced. "It feels like forever. We started right

after Christmas. I thought it would just happen. Instead of announcing we were trying, I wanted to announce my pregnancy, so I waited to tell you." She gave a derisive snort. "Shows how arrogant I can be."

"It'll happen. Be patient." Lisa studied the misery in Ginger's eyes as her friend nodded, not in agreement, but as though she'd heard such encouragement before. Lisa frowned. "What's really wrong?"

Ginger's eyes closed. When she opened them again, tears glistened. "Sex has become a chore," she whispered. "We don't make love now, we try to make a baby. It's a duty."

"I'm so sorry." Lisa rose and hugged Ginger.

"Kyle—" Ginger gulped. "It's like he hates me."

"Don't be ridiculous." Lisa winced at the severity of her words. "I mean, he obviously adores you. I've seen you together. You don't try to have a baby with someone you hate."

"He blames me for not conceiving."

Lisa drew back and looked in Ginger's face. "Has he said that?"

Ginger shook her head. "It's all in what he doesn't say. The way he looks at me."

"Gin, the way I remember this, it's a two-person activity."

Ginger's fingers twisted together on the table. "We're going to a fertility specialist next week."

"So soon?"

"It's been a few months. My gynecologist recommended it, just to eliminate possibilities."

Lisa bit her lip, staring at Ginger's downcast head. Never having had trouble conceiving, Lisa could only imagine her friend's torment. She'd like to have a few words with Kyle. Pressuring Ginger wouldn't help matters. He shouldn't put all the responsibility on her.

Ginger left soon after, wanting to get home to spend time with Kyle that didn't involve conception. Lisa checked the clock, then pushed to her feet and rummaged through her cupboard for lunch ideas.

During lunch, Lisa stared at her children picking at their tuna casserole and squabbling about who got control of the TV. What a blessing they were in her life. She'd do anything for them, including continuing the arrangement she had with her "fiancé."

As Bobby cleared the table and Abby scraped dishes and put them in the dishwasher, Lisa reconsidered Joe's predicament. He'd do anything for his family, too. Although she didn't approve of his methods, he'd cooked up this farce to protect his mother's health.

Maybe the time had come to rethink his dilemma as Ginger suggested. His efforts to appease his parents weren't much different than Lisa trying to raise her kids or Ginger trying to have a baby. It was all done for family. She couldn't fault him for that. The time had come to cut him some slack.

If she ever saw him again. By bedtime that night, he still hadn't called.

ON SUNDAY, Lisa still regretted walking out on dinner at the Rileys'. Catching up on her ironing while the children watched a movie upstairs, she berated herself for her cowardice. Why had she let Alice push her buttons? The older woman had gently bullied her into saying she'd marry Joe.

She should have just told them the truth about the charade. Joe would have gotten in deep parental hot water, but he was a big boy. If he'd stood up to his parents to begin with, she wouldn't be in this mess.

Yeah, right. Who was she to talk? She hadn't stood up to their pressure very well, either, and she wasn't even their flesh and blood. Joe couldn't run away as she had.

Lisa folded a pair of Abby's jeans as a knock sounded at the door. Her breath caught. Had she conjured Joe just by thinking of him? Perhaps he'd come to reassure her about her upcoming work for his company.

She ran her damp palms down her clothes, feeling self-conscious. A brief glance in the mirror confirmed she looked like a housemaid. She sighed and tucked her loose hair behind her ears, straightened her blouse and took a deep, calming breath. It didn't work. Her heart galloped; her palms remained damp. With a grimace she tried to turn into a welcoming smile, she opened the door.

Alice Riley smiled back at her.

With tremendous effort, Lisa kept from banging her forehead against the door frame. Why couldn't these extremely nice people leave her alone?

"Hello, Mrs. Riley. How are you feeling?" Lisa asked, firing the first salvo. Alice looked healthy enough.

Alice beamed. "Better, thank you. I hope you don't mind my stopping by like this. He said I should."

Lisa mentally ducked as Alice returned fire.

"Joe said you should drop by?" Lisa ground her teeth. She was going to kill him.

"No, no. Joe said I should mind my own business."

Surprise darted through Lisa.

"Mike said I should come by," Alice continued. "He said I drove him crazy with my pacing and muttering and talking about you all the time, and I should just come over and speak my piece. Get it off my chest."

Oh, great. Had Joe explained their relationship? Lisa still

couldn't believe he'd told his mother to mind her own business. At least he'd tried.

Alice cleared her throat. "May I come in?"

Lisa stepped back and opened the door wider. Might as well get this over with. It wasn't as though she didn't deserve a reprimand for trying to trick them.

They sat in the living room, facing each other across the coffee table, both perched on the edges of their chairs.

"I'm glad you came by," Lisa said, which wasn't a complete lie. "I want to apologize for leaving the way I did the other evening."

Alice said nothing.

"It wasn't very polite of me." The silence stretched. Lisa heard the clock ticking, the kids' TV program droning upstairs, the occasional car passing on the street. She swallowed. "The situation was just so awkward. That doesn't make it right, of course, but maybe you can understand."

"Of course. We didn't intend to make you uncomfortable, my dear. We only wanted to know when you and Joe were getting married."

Lisa twisted her fingers together in her lap. She couldn't meet Alice's gaze.

"I want to apologize, for myself and for Mike. We shouldn't have been so pushy."

Lisa nodded her acceptance, then shook her head. "I should have told you all about it myself."

"So you know that Joe explained everything," Alice said. "I wasn't sure if you'd spoken to him yet."

Lisa glanced at her. Alice had taken the news of their deceit pretty well. Joe must have done some fast talking.

"We understand now," Alice continued. "Although, of course, the old sayings hold truest. Honesty is the best policy."

"I agree. I try to teach my children that." Her face heated, and she looked away. "Not that I've been a good example recently."

"Even knowing what I know now about you, I'm sure you're a good mother."

Lisa winced at the backhanded compliment, then blew out a deep breath. She was getting off far easier than she deserved. "You're being very gracious, Mrs. Riley."

"Well, as Joe pointed out, it's really none of my business."

Lisa blinked. That was all? Joe pointed out his love life was none of their business, and his folks had just backed off? What magic words had he discovered all of a sudden?

"It's water over the dam now," Alice said.

And that was the end of it?

Alice continued, "When Joe explained the situation to us, we understood why you can't marry him right away like we had hoped."

Lisa stilled. She couldn't marry him *right away?* As in, she could marry him later? He hadn't explained anything. She would kill him in the slowest, most painful way she could devise. Dread weighted her breathing. "Just what did Joe 'explain' to you?"

"Don't worry, dear. He didn't confide all the details. Some things we just filled in for ourselves."

That sounded like trouble. Lisa bit back a groan and asked again, "What did he tell you?"

Alice dropped her gaze. "Until yesterday, we had believed you were a widow."

Lisa's mouth dropped open. When she could draw breath, she said, "Joe told you my husband was dead?"

Not that she hadn't considered murdering Brad herself.

Alice shook her head. "Joe didn't say that. We just

assumed it. We never imagined he'd get involved with a—" she leaned forward "—divorced woman."

The way she whispered it brought a smile to Lisa's face. Although she toyed with the idea for a moment, she couldn't adjust to this image of herself. Her, Lisa Ann Thornton Meyer, a risqué woman. A sexpot. A risk to innocent young men.

Which certainly left out Joe.

"We don't approve of divorce," Alice said. "The divorce rate today is scandalous. It seems nobody takes their vows seriously anymore."

Lisa pursed her lips, considering Alice's condemnation.

"No offense, dear," the older woman said sweetly.

"Of course not."

"And we understand not all marriages are held holy."

She blinked at Alice, unsure whether that was her cue to fill in the details of her marriage.

"Under most circumstances, a marriage can be saved and made stronger." Alice's eyes lit. "But maybe yours wasn't like that?"

A definite prod for information. Alice sounded hopeful. Hoping Lisa's marriage had been bad enough to justify divorce? Lisa felt no inclination to explain.

This would be the perfect out. She was taboo, forbidden to Joe by his family's beliefs, which he'd never mentioned. If he couldn't marry her, she no longer had to carry out this farce. She reeled with good cheer.

"Joe explained you were gun-shy. If you need some time to adjust to the idea of marrying again, we understand."

So much for good cheer. Lisa could have wept.

Alice smiled maternally. "But Joe's a good man. He'll always stand by you."

Wanna bet?

He hadn't explained a thing to his parents, except that she was divorced, not widowed. By saying she wanted to wait, he'd as much as stated his intention to propose when he felt Lisa was ready.

Her moment of truth had arrived. Should she betray his parents by continuing the deceit or betray Joe by exposing it? Her intention to cut him some slack only extended to being more understanding, not necessarily to continue lying.

Minutes ticked by.

Lisa rubbed her temple. Should she tell Alice? There wasn't a right answer. She recalled Ginger's question of the day before. Which was the lesser of the two wrongs—to break a mother's heart about her only child's dishonest nature or to continue to mislead the Rileys?

Lisa had had her fill of lies with Brad. She needed to tell Alice, even if the truth hurt her. Taking a deep breath, Lisa crossed her fingers in her lap for luck. The childish gesture did nothing to bolster her confidence. "Mrs. Riley, there's something you should know about me and Joe."

Alice waved a hand at her. "You don't need to explain. Mike warned me to keep my nose out of Joe's sex life."

Lisa choked. She had no intention of discussing Joe's sex life, especially not with his mother. Not that Lisa knew anything about his sex life, and she'd bet the profits from her next catering job that his mom didn't, either.

"We raised him the best we could. I shouldn't have said anything at dinner. Mike reminded me Joe's a healthy young man, with…well, needs."

Lisa groaned to herself, missing Alice's next words. No way would she discuss Joe's *needs* with his mother. She had to stop this. "Mrs. Riley—"

"Oh, call me Alice, please. Unless you could bring yourself to call me Mom?"

Lisa's protest caught in her throat like a fish bone. She drew in a wheezy breath.

"I'm sorry," Alice rushed on. "It's too early for you to feel comfortable with that. Mike always says I rush things. Push too hard." She patted Lisa's knee. "Don't worry about it. We'll stick with Alice for now."

Lisa closed her eyes. No wonder Joe couldn't force himself to disappoint her. The woman could make a tornado change course. She opened her eyes to find Alice studying her intently.

The older woman blinked and stood, gripping her purse. "I'd better get back and see what Mike's up to today. He promised to pick up a load of fertilizer for my new plantings."

She turned at the door, her sharp eyes tracing over Lisa's face. "Do you know anything about manure, Lisa?"

"Uh, no. I'm not much of a gardener." A guilty glance at her front path confirmed that statement. "I've always wanted to have flowers along the walk there, but I don't have the magic touch."

"I'll give you a tip, shall I?"

Lisa didn't trust the older woman's polite manner. Her formal tone sounded like a warning shot. It contained too much control for this to be simple conversation. A little warily, Lisa said, "Sure, I'd like that."

"Manure helps things grow." She held Lisa's gaze. "You have to tolerate its unpleasant qualities, like its smell, in order to reap its benefits."

"Oh. Okay."

She leaned toward Lisa. "But too much manure can burn the tender roots and bring death."

Alice turned and ambled to her car while Lisa stood in shock. Had she just been threatened? No, that was silly. How could that little old lady possibly hurt her?

So what had she meant? Death? Manure?

Lisa's breath caught. Could Alice suspect Lisa and Joe's engagement was just a pile of...manure? If so, why would Alice go along with it? Did she have some fantasy that their pretense would become real?

Chapter Six

"I need to know where I stand," Lisa said to Joe when she walked into his office Monday morning. She'd paced all the previous night, worrying she'd also lost his company's catering contract when she'd lost her temper at his parents' house. He hadn't called to reassure her otherwise.

So there she waited, having faced down his secretary, Sue, the guardian of his calendar. But Lisa had growing children and was becoming well versed in countering evasion tactics. His pretty little secretary hadn't had a chance.

"What do you mean?" he asked.

"Am I still catering your company's party or not?"

He blinked. "Of course. We have a deal."

She almost wilted with relief. His confusion indicated he'd never considered canceling. Lisa could have kicked herself. She shouldn't assume he'd renege on their deal just because one man had been less than honorable about keeping his word.

And his vows.

"I'm sorry. I just worried after Friday night, you might think I'd failed my part of the bargain."

Joe shrugged. "It didn't go well, but that's hardly your

fault. Our agreement is you'll pretend we have a serious relationship. You're doing that."

"Even though I told your folks Abby and Bobby wouldn't be their grandchildren?" She could scarcely believe it.

"That wasn't the best choice of tactics, I agree, but my parents knew you'd spoken in the heat of the moment. At least, that's what they believed, not knowing our true circumstances."

"Yes," Lisa said, as she slid into a chair across the desk from him. "I gathered your mother thought our wedding is still on the horizon."

He froze. "What do you mean, you 'gathered' that?"

Lisa smirked and waited for him to figure it out on his own.

"She called you?" When Lisa made no reply, his eyes widened. "She came by? When?"

"Yesterday. She wanted to assure me she and your dad would be patient about us setting a date." Lisa arched an eyebrow. "After I get over my cold feet about marrying again, that is. You know how we divorcées are."

Joe flushed and cleared his throat. "Well, as to that. My mom had to take to her bed right after dinner Friday. She wasn't strong enough to get up until Sunday morning."

Lisa stared at him. "She did what?"

"Dad called me to help ease her mind. I had to say something." He ran a hand down his face, as though scrubbing away a memory. "I invented a reason for you to be hesitant about remarrying. It bought us some time."

She couldn't take it in. Mrs. Riley hadn't appeared to be ailing on Sunday. Her color looked good; her mind was sharp. Her tongue certainly had been. Had she finished eating dinner Friday before becoming "indisposed," Lisa wondered cynically. Her suspicions made her feel uncharitable, but Alice's behavior bordered on the dramatic. Maybe Joe wasn't the only Riley who could act. "I can't believe your mom was ill."

He nodded. "Her setback gave us a scare, but she's better now."

"No, I mean I can't believe she…" How to phrase this? What proof did she have? None Joe would accept. "She looked fine to me."

"I wish I'd known." He shook his head.

"It's okay." She smiled reassuringly, touched by his concern for her. "I handled it."

"I mean I wish I'd known she'd been out. What if she'd had a relapse while driving?"

Lisa clenched her jaw. So much for his support. "I doubt there was any danger of that happening."

"How can we know for sure? What was Dad thinking, letting her go out by herself?"

"I don't think he knew. Your mother mentioned he'd gone to the garden store."

Joe thrust a hand into his hair. "She sneaked out?"

"That's my guess."

"But why?" He speared her with a sharp glance. "What did you two have to talk about?"

"She apologized for misunderstanding the situation between us."

"What situation?" His eyes widened. "Our having sex?"

Lisa smiled. "Partly. Trust me, I didn't let her go on too long about you being 'a healthy young man with needs.'"

His face went red, and she struggled to withhold her laughter. She shouldn't torment him, but an inner devil made her want to pay him back for what she'd endured talking about the same subject with his mom.

"Oh, my God," he muttered.

"Yeah, that was pretty much my thought, too." She sobered. "Joe, I think she's on to us."

"I doubt it."

His dismissive tone set her on edge. "She warned me about too much manure bringing death."

"Wha-at?"

Lisa relayed the conversation to him, after which he shook his head. "Sounds like gardening advice."

Men. They could be so dense. "I think she suspects."

"Trust me, Lisa, if my mother suspected anything, we wouldn't have to wonder about it." He cleared his throat. "I wanted to apologize, too."

"About what?"

"The sex talk at the dinner table." He swallowed. "I'm sorry my folks started in on that."

No doubt Joe felt cornered by his mother's totally wrong interpretation of his acting. Alice may have taken his attention to Lisa seriously, but she knew better.

"Don't worry about it. Your act may be a tad overdone, but the idea was to make your mom and dad believe we're seriously involved. I know it's just a pretense. That you're not…"

For once she stopped herself, leaving the sentence hanging. The less said, the better.

"That I'm not what?"

She rolled her eyes. Couldn't he leave it alone?

"Not what?" he demanded.

"Not really attracted to me."

"Not *really* attracted?"

"No. Not in reality, I should say."

Joe stood. Lisa did, as well, scooting behind her chair, closer to the door. She didn't like the glint in his eye.

"Why would you think that?" he asked.

"It's all a charade. I just want you to know I haven't forgotten what we're doing."

"So you don't feel anything like that toward me?" He walked closer.

Lisa stepped away. "Joe, don't be silly. It's just a game."

"To whom?"

She almost giggled. "Well, maybe 'game' isn't the right word." She took another step back. "I don't want you to think I don't care about your mother's feelings."

"Oh, *her* feelings you care about."

"And your dad's, of course." Her back encountered the wall.

"I'm so glad," he said, his tone belying his words. "At least you care about someone's feelings."

"What do you mean?"

He braced his palms on the wall on either side of her head. Lisa swallowed as the possessive gesture and the warmth of his body heated hers. "Me. My feelings."

"Yours?"

"A guy doesn't exactly like to hear the woman he's interested in isn't attracted to him 'in reality.'"

She put up a hand in protest. It landed on his chest. His hard, warm, solidly male chest. "Joe, come on. You're getting carried away here. I never said I wasn't—"

She caught herself before she could admit her attraction.

His eyebrows rose. "Please continue. This could be interesting."

"You're forgetting the arrangement," she said, embarrassed to have to spell it out. "You aren't attracted to me. It's just that you have to pretend to be."

He smiled.

She shivered, all too aware of him.

"Is that so?" he asked.

She nodded her head.

"Let's just see, shall we?" Joe lowered his head and took her mouth with his.

Lisa had to lock her knees to avoid melting to the floor. His lips moved on hers as though he had all day to convince her of his interest. His intoxicating male attention totally focused on her made her tremble. She hadn't been kissed so intently in longer than she could remember.

He looked into her eyes, which she feared showed her feelings.

"I started thinking Friday night," he said just before he brushed his lips across hers again.

"Hmm?" was all the response she could make.

"When my mom was lying there in bed, pressing me for a wedding date."

Lisa's eyes flew open, fully alert. What had he done now? Warily she asked, "Yes?"

"I thought maybe just telling her the truth would be the right thing to do."

Lisa's stomach knotted, with dread this time. They wouldn't have an excuse to see each other again, other than his company's party. She swallowed her disappointment, knowing this was the more honorable path. "I've always said being honest would be best."

"But then I realized I want to keep seeing you. So I didn't tell her anything."

He wanted to start dating? Her head spun. She considered dating Joe as she searched his expression. She was certainly attracted to him, but could she trust another man again?

About to say she'd be willing to try it, Lisa hesitated, still unsure.

"I was thinking…" he started.

"Yes?" Ready to jump out of her skin, she could barely contain her nerves.

"Since we're already seeing each other, I thought maybe it was time to take this relationship to its next logical level."

"I don't understand."

"We're pretty combustible." He kissed her, obviously not noticing her sudden lack of response. "It's clear we'll end up as lovers, sooner or later. I'm thinking sooner sounds good."

"I see." She could only stare.

"I see, as in 'yes'?"

"No."

His brow furrowed. "I don't mean right now, this minute. More like this weekend probably. I don't have a meeting, so unless something comes up, either night would work."

Great. He could fit in an affair around business. She'd be angry if she wasn't so vibrantly turned on. She also understood his dedication to his work. Of course multimillion-dollar deals would take precedence over sex.

Lisa eased herself out of his arms. He let her go, the reluctance he felt evident in the trail of his hands across her skin.

"We'd go out to dinner first," he said. "I'll find a quiet, romantic restaurant."

She smiled at his attempt to persuade her. She didn't need dinner in a romantic restaurant.

"With candlelight and music."

She didn't need either of those things, either. "I can't."

"Why not?"

She simply shook her head. She needed some sense of commitment, the probability of them having a future together.

"Is it the kids?" he asked. "Because I do have an apartment, you know. I wasn't expecting you to just tell them to go play and then lock your bedroom door to play with me."

Joe could have kicked himself when she winced. Could he be more crass? He'd always been a smooth talker, with women and in business, but his self-assurance left the building when Lisa measured him with her lake-blue eyes. From the first day when she'd discovered his plan to appease his mom's worries, Lisa had looked at him and found him wanting.

He should just shelve this idea and find a willing woman. One without kids or hang-ups about fudging the truth. For some reason, he'd set his sights on Lisa. He really was insane.

"I'm sorry, Joe," she said. She opened the door and glanced back at him, her eyes huge in her face. "More sorry than you'll know."

Joe crossed the room and sank down in his leather chair. He tilted back, putting his feet on his desk. He'd take a minute, no more, to catch his breath. But he found his breath constricted in his chest. Lisa didn't want to have an affair with him. How had he misinterpreted the signals?

Maybe she hadn't been sending signals, he thought with a self-derisive snort. Perhaps he'd been deluding himself, seeing what he wanted to see.

Then he recalled their kiss. No, the softness of her lips, the tightness of her arms, the urgent press of her body all told the same story. She'd been more than receptive to his embrace.

He didn't get it. What was more natural than advancing to the inevitable next step?

Joe flung himself forward, planted his feet squarely on the floor and picked up a pen and file folder to get down to work. After fifteen minutes of staring at the same document and not seeing a word or symbol he could decipher, he gave it up, flinging the pen across his desk in disgust. With more haste than he'd admit to if challenged, he left the cavernous solitude of his office and headed to Research and Development. Work called like a siren, luring him not onto the rocks, but into a comfortable sanctuary.

"Hey, Dylan," he called at his partner's door.

Dylan's office had a huge window for its fourth wall, overlooking the research teams at their computers. He liked nothing better than fixing things, and more often than not, could be found with a team, poring over figures.

Joe's forte leaned more toward securing the bids, governmental and private, to keep the company in business. Today, however, he longed for a complex technical meltdown to distract him.

Dylan finished a notation and eyed him. "What's up?"

Joe shrugged and loosened his tie, feeling claustrophobic. Dylan never had that problem. He seldom wore a tie or jacket. Even now, several buttons were undone and his shirt-sleeves rolled up.

"Is it that woman? The caterer?" When Joe jerked in surprise, Dylan smiled. "I buzzed you earlier. Sue told me the lady had come, uninvited."

Joe scowled.

"I thought it an odd phrase, too. Does Sue have a thing for you?"

"She's married."

Dylan tapped a pen on his desk.

"Sue's protective, is all."

"If you're sure."

Joe nodded.

"So if your woman problem isn't your secretary, can I assume it's your caterer?"

"You're a riot."

Dylan smiled and laced his hands behind his head. "Tell me."

"I suggested we go to my place sometime this weekend."

"For sex."

"Yeah."

Dylan clutched his chest in mock astonishment. "And she didn't fall at your feet?"

"It was a reasonable offer."

"But not a romantic one." Dylan shook his head. "Joe, Joe, Joe. You're off your game, man. What's happened to the old smooth-talker we all depend on?"

"I'm not having trouble wooing clients."

"Just women?"

"Just Lisa."

"Ah. So what makes her different?"

Joe glowered at the knowing smile on his partner's face. "She has kids."

"And?"

"We have fewer opportunities to be together. I can't exactly jump her in front of her children."

"But you'd like to jump her?"

"It's not just sex," Joe said in his defense. He didn't like the way Dylan made it sound. "Our relationship is complex."

"Because she's catering our party in July?"

"Among other things." Joe paced the office, stopping to stare through the glass. He'd come to Dylan because his partner excelled at solving problems. Taking a deep breath, he admitted, "We're pretending to have a relationship to get my mom off my back."

Dead silence filled the room.

Joe turned to find Dylan staring at him.

"You're a real ass, you know that, don't you?"

Joe shrugged.

Dylan shook his head. "And now it's more than pretend?"

"She's interesting."

"And good-looking."

Joe glared. "I saw her first."

"Fair enough. So what are you going to do about her?"

"You've dated moms before, right?"

"A few."

"How do you handle the sex thing?" When Dylan grinned, Joe pitched a paper clip at his head. "You know what I mean."

"Same way you do with an unattached woman. You build up to it."

Joe nodded. "Makes sense. Thanks, Dyl."

When Joe reached the door, Dylan called out, "Hey, let me know when you blow it with her. I might give her a call."

Joe flipped him the bird and ignored his friend's laughter following him down the hall.

"HEY, MOM," ABBY CALLED from the kitchen doorway the next evening. "Guess who's here for dinner."

Lisa couldn't guess. She was up to her elbows in lasagna. She hoped it wasn't Abby's too-perfect friend, Sally Turner, of the upcoming concert fame. Although she'd like to have a stern talk with Sally's parents, she didn't know what she'd say to the girl. Lisa couldn't relate to a person who had everything—well, everything except parents with common sense.

Fortunately, or maybe not, Lisa didn't have to deal with Sally. When she glanced over her shoulder to greet her guest, it turned out to be Joe, looking good enough to eat in jeans worn nearly white with age and a red polo shirt displaying his tanned, muscled arms. Lisa rolled her eyes to heaven and went back to layering lasagna.

"Mom? Did you hear me?" Abby said. "Mr. Riley said he'd been invited to dinner."

That made her turn to face him.

His smile shouldn't have heated her skin. She shouldn't have noticed the uncertainty lurking in his gaze or found it endearing. She could definitely do without endearing. She narrowed her eyes. "You were invited?"

He shrugged. "Not for tonight, specifically, but after I had spaghetti here, I'm sure you said we'd do it again."

Abby frowned. "Oh, I thought you meant tonight."

Lisa tried a reassuring smile but felt its stiffness and gave up the effort. "It's no big deal, honey." She sent a pointed glare his way. "Mr. Riley misled you, but I don't mind if he stays."

After splitting a look between the two adults, Abby sprang from the door back to the living room with youthful energy. And no doubt with a measure of relief.

Joe stepped into the kitchen. Lisa spun away. She wanted to launch herself into his arms, to rekindle the passion that had flared in his office and hadn't quite died, no matter how often she doused the embers with common sense. She wanted to go up in flames.

She also wanted to bang a skillet over his head for tormenting her.

Instead, she assembled the lasagna in silence, only acknowledging his presence when she gestured him away from the oven to put the meal in to bake.

"I know things went wrong between us yesterday," Joe said finally. "Thanks for letting me stay."

"As if I had a choice. You bamboozled my daughter. If I'd made a fuss, she'd have felt responsible."

His shoulders shifted. Was he squirming? She turned away with the excuse of washing her hands, glad if he felt guilty for using Abby.

"I want you."

Lisa took a deep breath, reaching for inner calmness and missing by a mile. His admission thrilled her. Darn it.

Joe stepped up behind her, close enough for her to feel his warmth, his breath on her neck, his masculine scent wrapping around her. His hands cupped her shoulders. "I hope you want me…to stay for dinner, at least."

She forced herself not to lean against him, no matter how she yearned to rest her head on his chest and feel his arms envelop her.

"I'd hate to lose our friendship," he said.

She straightened. "What friendship?"

He turned her to face him. His eyes shone a deep serious blue. "The one we've started. The one I hope will build as we get to know one another better."

She looked away.

His fingers on her chin brought her back. "Let's make sure we're on the same page here."

"What page?"

"This one." Then his lips brushed hers, not demanding, but sweet and sincere. Not playing or coaxing her into something deeper, something she could have refused.

His mouth shared, greeted, praised. He didn't take or command. When he ended the kiss, his eyes gleamed, not with triumph, which she could have scorned and hardened herself against, but with pleasure, which she could only revel in.

"It'll never work." Her voice came out croaky.

A lopsided smile answered her. "Not with that attitude." He stepped back and rubbed his hands. "Now, you need me to make the salad or something? I'm no Chef Boyardee, but I think I could manage garlic bread."

She handed him lettuce and a serving bowl. Before she realized his intent, he took the lettuce from the spinner, rinsed her already cleaned and dried lettuce, and tore it into pieces. Lisa almost laughed aloud. Not exactly Chef Boyardee? He didn't even recognize a salad spinner.

He was adorable. If only…

Lisa reined in her thoughts. She'd had the fairy tale with Brad—not that marrying due to a teen pregnancy qualified as a fairy tale, but they'd had good years—then that had turned into a bitter nightmare. He'd moved on when a younger, prettier girl caught his eye. Who was to say Joe wouldn't do the same? And they weren't even talking long-term commitment, just lust. With kids to consider, she couldn't indulge in a brief affair.

"I can't."

His hands stilled.

The words erupted without thought, but she didn't call them back. She might regret the missed opportunity with Joe, the passion she'd barely tasted with him, but the decision placated her cautious personality.

He continued with his task. "I understand."

Joe finished and dried his hands on a towel, then so quickly she didn't have time to protest, he pinned her against the counter with his body. He trailed his tongue up the side of her neck and lingered to suck the cord of her throat, like an amorous vampire. Then he stepped away.

He left the kitchen and went to talk to Bobby about some sport, something where being offside constituted a foul.

He'd just agreed not to go forth with an affair, then sent her blood racing. If she wasn't offside, she was definitely off balance. But did what she yearned to do with Joe constitute a foul?

For the remainder of the evening, Joe kept his hands to himself, confirming her belief. The kiss ended it. They'd just be business associates from here on out.

Although she wanted—badly—to have a fling with Joe, she wasn't so sure she could have him in her life. For that, she'd have to trust him, and she doubted she could do that again. She stabbed at the lasagna on her plate, cursing Brad for making her so wary. This was another thing her ex-husband had taken from her. In comparison, her money problems seemed simple to fix. The blow to her self-esteem would take some work.

"Mom, did you have a fight with Mr. Riley again?" Bobby asked.

Lisa jerked, almost flinging lasagna from her fork. "What makes you think that?"

Bobby glared at Joe, who looked as blank-faced with surprise as she felt. "You've been pouting all through dinner."

"Pouting?" She fought a smile at the simple six-year-old observation.

"We weren't fighting," Joe said.

Bobby glared at him.

"You have been quiet, Mom," Abby said, darting a glance between the two adults.

"I was thinking hard." Lisa checked their expressions. "You all were getting along well enough."

Bobby leaped from his chair. "But I don't want to get along with him if you're mad at him."

"I'm not mad at him."

"I don't intend to make your mom unhappy," Joe said at the same time.

Lisa forced a smile to her face as Bobby tried to gauge Joe's sincerity. She appreciated her son's show of support, but worried about the outburst during what had been a calm meal. "Sit down, honey, and finish your dinner."

Bobby's unpredictable temper had improved only a little after enrolling in the school program. He avoided Arnold in class and didn't fight. He and Joe had talked peacefully enough before dinner, but now this outburst. He progressed a step and a half forward, one step back. But, she mused, there was progress, however minimal.

With obvious reluctance, Bobby slid back onto his chair.

After dinner, Joe said his goodbyes to the kids and led the way to the porch. The soft night air cooled her skin and cleared her mind. Inhaling a lungful, she asked, "Why did you come over tonight?"

"To build up to seducing you."

Lisa snapped to attention, not expecting this. His answer dried her throat and hurried her heartbeat.

He pulled her close. His breath whispered against her hair. "To hold you and touch you, feel your body against mine. To start convincing you to have an affair with me."

She gasped in amazement. Joe moved in on her, caressing her lips with his own, mating their tongues. Lisa's head spun. Her breathing filled with his scent. She wanted to engulf him, with her arms, with her mouth, with her body. When his hands cupped her bottom, pulling her closer to his arousal, she moaned her agreement.

Then he turned away and walked to his car.

She ran a hand through her hair. "Where are you going?"

"Home," he called over his shoulder.

She hurried after him. "Why?"

"I have to leave." He slammed his car door, and the engine roared to life, although he pulled away from the curb sedately enough.

Why had he done that, aroused her to acquiescence then simply left? What would she do when she saw him again?

JOE PASSED a restless night tormented by need and wondering if he should have walked away from Lisa. He'd only meant to kiss her good-night. Build up to an affair. Damn Dylan and his advice. The moment Joe got around Lisa, he wanted her in his arms. Build slowly? Yeah, right.

Now he watched his father turn a length of wood on his lathe. The slight breeze blowing into the garage made it a nice day to hang out in his dad's workshop after work on Wednesday, sipping beer and shooting bull. He felt himself wind down after a tedious day at the office. Watching his dad work sure beat trying to deal with his mom.

Joe took a deep breath. His head hurt, and not just because he'd had five beers when he got home from dinner at Lisa's the night before. Dealing with his mother strained his patience. He thought about their earlier confrontation.

"You are not to get involved in my relationships anymore. Have we got this straight, Mom?" He'd held his mother's gaze, hoping she didn't collapse. He scanned her face for signs of stress.

"I don't appreciate your tone." She looked at her husband, but for once, he withheld his support.

"And I don't appreciate your interference."

"Joe," his father said quietly.

"Sorry, Dad."

His dad stared at him.

Joe hunched his shoulders in the face of his father's rebuke. "Sorry, Mom."

She smiled. "That's better. Now, why don't we have some dinner."

Joe didn't believe for one second his mother would stop meddling. He could only hope she'd find something else to occupy her for a while. He wanted to make some headway with Lisa.

He watched his father's large, blunt hands as he did some fancy scrollwork with the circular saw. Those upper-management hands had acquired scratches and scars when his dad had retired and taken up his hobby.

His dad intercepted his gaze. "What are you staring at?"

Joe shook his head. "I'm always amazed you haven't lost a finger. You ever consider needlepoint?"

His dad chuckled. "Sometimes you have to go through a painful period of adjustment when you try something new."

Don't I know it.

"I just had to adjust to the saw wanting to send the wood its own way." He stood back and wiped his wrist across his forehead, frowning at the wood. "I can't tell you what it means to your mom and me that you're thinking about getting married."

Joe clenched his teeth, searching for patience. This constant marriage talk drove him crazy. It wouldn't be so bad if he were actually engaged. Except then he'd be engaged.

"Are you worried about becoming a father?" his own father asked.

"A father?" Joe echoed, feeling sucker punched. He swallowed. He'd felt suffocated the night before at dinner, striving for conversation with the kids. At the beginning, he'd held his own with Bobby, talking sports, then he'd floundered, devoid of topics. How would he do with kids full-time? "Yeah, I guess."

"Usually a couple gets some good years in before they have kids to fight about. It's different from when you were a boy."

"What do you mean?"

His father sighed. "I wasn't there very much. That's the way things were back then, Joe. Dads went to work, and moms took care of the house and the family. Dads just whipped the kids into shape when they got into trouble."

Joe smiled. "Yeah, I was always real worried about you whipping me."

His dad chuckled. "Okay, so I'm not a heavy-handed guy."

Joe shook his head. "It was all in the way you looked at me. Sometimes when you were disappointed, it just about killed me." He took a swig of beer, uneasy with laying open his feelings.

"Nevertheless, I didn't offer you a very good role model. Just look at you."

Joe's mouth dropped open. "What's wrong with me?"

"You can't see it." His dad rested a hand on Joe's shoulder. "But you're a workaholic, son."

Joe stepped away, and his dad's hand dropped to his side. He felt the unfair sting of his father's indictment.

"I know that's hard to hear," his dad said, "but don't get discouraged. You can overcome it. Things are different now. You don't have to work all the time. You get to be with your kids."

"Huh?" Too much was being thrown at Joe; he couldn't catch a breath. Spending time with his kids and not getting to work? That didn't appeal to him, at all. Work was his life. He and Dylan had built Riley and Ross Electronics into a force to be reckoned with, whether they were located in the

Midwest or on the West Coast. How could he cut back on his hours? "I don't think that's the kind of father I'll be."

His dad held his gaze. "Son, I want you to think about that real hard. I have a lot of regrets. Not being there for you, not making your ball games. There were a lot of things I couldn't go to, plays and events at school—"

"I was never in the school play."

"That's not the point. The point is when you're a dad nowadays, you get to take off. They even have paternity leave, for gosh sakes, so you can stay home with a baby."

Joe's knees turned to water. He had to force himself to remain upright. *Stay at home with a baby?* The hollow feeling in his stomach grew.

"Haven't you thought about having kids of your own? Other than Lisa's I mean."

"Well, uh, I..." Joe blustered. "She has two already. I doubt she'd want more."

When his father turned away, Joe felt the weight of his disappointment. "Dad, it's not like I need to continue the line or anything. That's kind of old-fashioned."

His dad ran a hand over the sawn wood. "I'd like to see some more Rileys in the world. So, sue me."

Joe sighed. To make his folks happy, now he not only had to get married, he had to have a baby, too?

Lisa would love that.

JOE SAT IN HIS OFFICE the next day, restless and unable to work. His dad had missed out on his life? Okay, so he hadn't attended most of Joe's games, and Joe had done his homework with his mother while his dad worked late, but there was more to being a father than struggling through algebra and cheering on your kid.

Unable to sit still, Joe wandered out to his secretary's office. "How're things going, Sue?"

She glanced up from her computer screen. "Did you need something?"

"No, I'm just thinking while I walk. Don't let me bother you."

"Okay." Sue turned back to her monitor.

Joe meandered around her office, then poured some coffee. He brushed a big broad-leaved plant over by the chairs where clients waited, and he thought maybe he'd get one for his office. Except then Sue would have to water it because he didn't really want to take care of any plants.

Maybe that was the problem. He didn't want to bother.

No, he was thinking about plants here, not kids. This thing with his dad had driven him crazy. Him, a workaholic? That was a hoot. He didn't know where his dad came up with that one.

He stalked back into his office, beyond irritated. Time to get back to work.

He'd probably have kids someday. When he was ready, maybe six or seven years from now. In the meantime, maybe he could do something with Abby and Bobby. Get used to having kids around. It would give him an idea how he'd do in the future.

He didn't know if he'd be a good dad, and that scared him. He was always good at things. He could build a company, move it to the middle of America, in a town ninety-eight percent of the country didn't know existed, and still have it thrive. He was *that good*.

He could build a business, but could he build a family? He'd start with Lisa's. Test-marketing with her kids before he took on a bigger commitment one day made sense.

Commitment? Joe winced a bit as the word hit him.

He had to figure out the first step to becoming a father. Not the usual way, he thought with a chuckle. He'd love to have sex with Lisa, but so far, no go.

He turned to his computer and started typing. He called the file Fatherhood. The first page: Ways to Win Over the Kids. As he made his list, he deleted some ideas right away, remembering the video game system debacle.

When he finished, he leaned back and stretched. Now his plan to get his mom off his back had two parts. Part A: He'd ease his parents' minds about him being alone. Part B: He'd see if he could be a good father someday.

Joe smiled, sure of his next few steps.

Chapter Seven

Lisa opened her door Saturday morning with a sense of dread. She had a sinking feeling who she'd find at her door so early. Sure enough, Joe stood on her porch, exuding good cheer. She didn't know where he got the nerve.

"Hi," he said with a smile charismatic enough to beguile, if one wanted to be led down that path, which Lisa assured herself she didn't. She still ached from unfulfilled passion.

"I know I'm not expected, but I thought we could all go somewhere together if you don't have plans already. Maybe the zoo."

Lisa stared at him.

"My secretary says it's better to go on a family outing on a weekday to avoid the crowds, but since the kids are still in school, we'll just have to deal with it."

She eyed him warily. "A family outing?"

"Sure. I even packed a picnic."

"You?"

"Yes, me."

His smile formed edges that pleased Lisa no end. Why should he always get his way?

"What do you say?"

He'd already been around Abby and Bobby, so she couldn't argue he was breaking their agreement. Unable to come up with a good reason not to go, she sighed. "Let's ask the kids."

The kids listened to his offer with equal wariness.

"The zoo's for babies," Bobby, who loved the zoo, declared with a petulant expression.

Lisa hoped Bobby wouldn't have an outburst now.

"The zoo's not all bad," Abby cut in before Lisa could chide him for his rudeness. "But there are places more fun."

"Such as?" Joe took the bait.

"Worlds of Fun," the children chorused.

Joe's shoulders drooped infinitesimally before resetting in a firm line. "Fine, we'll go there."

Abby squealed. Huge smiles lit both kids' faces.

"Not there. We can't impose like that." Lisa searched for a reason as all three frowned at her. She couldn't spend all day with Joe, and he would hate it.

"It's too expensive," Abby confided to Joe in a resigned tone that broke Lisa's heart and tore at her pride.

"I can afford it," Joe said.

"We couldn't ask you to—" Lisa said.

"You didn't ask," he replied.

"Why can't we ask?" Bobby wondered. "Isn't that how you find out stuff?"

Lisa blew out a breath, feeling pressured. "I'm sure Mr. Riley didn't intend to stay out all day. An amusement park is exhausting, even for kids."

Joe's lips quirked. "I believe I can keep up."

"He can rest at Oceans of Fun," Abby offered. "It's hot enough for swimming."

"Sorry, the water park isn't open until Memorial Day." Thank goodness. She'd never expose that much of her body to Joe after he'd walked away from her, plainly expressing his disinterest.

"Aw, I wanted to go swimming," Bobby said.

Abby nudged him. "Don't whine or she'll say no."

"She's already said no," Bobby reminded her.

"Only to the water park."

"Oh." Bobby's face lit. "I can be ready in two minutes. Bet I beat Abby." He bounded up the stairs, laughing with a seldom-heard delight.

"No, you won't," Abby called as she ran after him. "'Cause I just need shoes."

"And sun scream," he called from his room, his voice muffled. "We don't want to burn."

"Sun 'scream'?" Joe smiled. "I didn't think of that."

Lisa slumped on the couch, outmaneuvered. "That's not surprising. You're not exactly used to going out with children."

"Thanks for being such a good sport."

She frowned. "Did I agree to this?"

He sat across from her. "You don't want to disappoint the kids now. They're looking forward to it."

"We haven't been in a while," she said, biting her lip at the huge understatement. They hadn't been able to afford to do much of anything in the past year. "I should probably pack more food. You don't realize how much those two can eat."

"I packed a substantial lunch, full of nutritious foods and some goodies," he added with a smile. "If we need more drinks or anything, we'll just buy them there."

She rolled her eyes. "You have no idea what they charge at these amusement parks."

"Relax."

Easy for him to say, with his bank account firmly in the

black. She clenched her teeth. How dare he come here offering her children a treat she couldn't afford, acting as though nothing had happened between them, that he hadn't set her on fire then heartlessly vamoosed? If she didn't know better, she'd think he was trying to integrate himself into her life. Since she did know better, she had to suspect his motives. "What are you up to?"

"What do you mean?" His expression radiated innocence.

"Don't think you'll get away with it."

"With what?"

"With—" She waved her hand in the air. "With whatever this is you're doing."

"I'm just taking your family out for the day. Spending time together, getting to know them better."

"Why?"

Joe started, and his confident expression slipped. "Why shouldn't I? No, no." He held up a hand as she started to speak, full of reasons. "Let's just say because I want to."

Lisa narrowed her eyes. She'd been outfoxed enough for one day. "Let's just say that, or is it the truth?"

"What a cynic. Shouldn't you put on some sun 'scream,' too? I wouldn't want that soft skin to burn. Then you'd be even more untouchable."

She blinked at his words and the sensual gleam in his eyes. A compliment followed by what? An accusation she was aloof? Hadn't he been paying attention when she incinerated in his arms?

Joe shifted, his expression becoming more serious. "About the other night."

"I don't want to talk about it."

"But I do. I need to tell you how difficult it was for me to leave. I thought it the best thing to do, under the circumstances."

"I'm sure you had your reasons," Lisa answered, trying to salvage some self-esteem. Her fingers dug into the cushion.

"Besides being in your front yard, on display for the neighbors, with the kids able to watch from inside or walk up to us any second? I didn't think you really wanted to make love."

"Then you're not as bright as you think you are." She squeezed her eyes shut, regretting the words as soon as they emerged. Oh, jeez. Had she really just admitted how turned-on she'd been?

Joe's confident smile singed her pride even more. "I know you wanted me physically, and if we'd snuck behind a bush or hidden in my car, we'd have been like butter on toast."

Lisa gasped with outrage. Not that it wasn't true…

"But then what?"

She blinked, not keeping up, wanting to blast him for his remark, but distracted by this new attack. "Then what, what?"

"Then you would have been sorry."

"I'm so—" She bit her lip, suspecting Joe could guess her unspoken words. She needed to keep her mouth shut if she wanted to retain any dignity at all. She had to get him to drop this subject altogether.

"I don't want you to regret it," he said.

"So you were being a gentleman?"

He grinned. "No, I just ran like the hounds of hell were at my heels. I didn't figure out why until later."

Lisa sat still, disarmed by his honesty. She *would* have regretted it, that was the killer, regretted doing it even more than she now regretted missing out on it. Joe's observation was dead-on, and she disliked him for knowing her so well. "How do you think today's outing is going to overcome this reluctance you think I feel?"

He shrugged. A totally frustrating response.

With a sigh, she pushed to her feet. "I'll get the sunscreen."

THE DAY COULD BE DEEMED a success, depending on what one wanted from it. For Abby and Bobby, the trip outshone their expectations. The rides were higher, faster and more thrilling than they'd anticipated, even in the little kid section of the park. The food tasted better, and the shows were more entertaining. They'd watched TV commercials and listened to their friends talk about how much fun the park could offer but hadn't held much hope of going themselves. Lisa winced each time one of them voiced the thought. Bobby didn't remember being there before, and Abby's memories had faded to shadowy impressions.

Lisa's heart ached with joy as she watched her kids. If she occasionally struggled with guilt over not being able to bring them herself, she still wanted them to have this treat.

For Joe, who knew? Since she didn't understand what he wanted from the outing, she couldn't tell if he'd gotten his money's worth or not.

And he was spending money. The place acted as a vacuum, sucking the cash out of his wallet before she could intervene. Although she'd put her foot down regarding souvenirs, he still spent more than she felt comfortable with.

He'd been a prince to the kids, riding the faster and scarier rides with them, buying drinks and snacks, charming them with his easygoing disposition. He'd even smoothed over a tantrum when Bobby failed the height requirement on one of the roller coasters Lisa took Abby on.

It was over their picnic lunch that Joe blew it. Not allowed to take food into the park, they'd spread a blanket under a tree in the parking area, sharing the grass with another family.

"I think Sally has been here a couple times this season already," Abby said, staring at her sandwich. "They opened last weekend."

And yet Sally claimed to have already come several times? It broke Lisa's heart to see Abby taken in by such a girl.

"Please," Lisa cut in. "It's too nice a day to discuss Sally Turner."

"Who's Sally Turner?" Joe asked.

Lisa sighed.

"She's this really cool girl at school," Abby informed him with a light in her eyes to match her smile. "She has all the best clothes and the newest CDs. Everyone likes her." She glowered at her mother. "Well, almost everyone."

Joe glanced at Lisa. "Why don't you like her?"

"She's spoiled. She has no sense of values. Her parents have no clue—"

"Oh, Mom, you don't even know her."

"That's a good point," Lisa said. "You've never brought her over to play. You've never been friends, let alone close friends. Now all of a sudden, she's the best thing since sliced bread."

"Since what?" Bobby asked.

"Why would Sally want to come to our house?" Abby overrode him. "She has all these great video games and her own rec room for having friends over. It has a refrigerator, a microwave and everything. Her parents aren't even allowed to go in when she has friends with her, unless they knock."

"Sounds like a fun place," Joe said.

Lisa glared at him. "That's the problem. It's undersupervised. Her parents 'aren't allowed' in? What kind of parents would permit that with an eight-year-old?"

"Fun ones. And she's already nine." Abby caught her mother's glare and subsided into a pout.

"That's not 'fun,' Abby," Lisa said. "That's being irresponsible. Which is why you're not going to her party."

"Oh," Joe said. "That's what all this is about." He smiled at Abby. "You girls are going to behave yourselves, aren't you?"

Abby blushed and nodded, studying her hands folded in her lap.

"There," he appealed to Lisa, "you have Abby's word she'll behave as well when she's away from home as you would expect. She's a good kid, right?"

Lisa shut her eyes and took a deep breath. She appreciated his efforts to befriend her daughter, even though he didn't know the circumstances. "This isn't about trusting Abby. This is about the kind of household which allows eight- and nine-year-olds to go across the state overnight to see a concert."

Joe blinked. He glanced at Abby, who didn't look up, then at Bobby, who had started playing Batman with the drink cups. Finally he turned back to Lisa and cleared his throat. "Who's playing?"

Lisa ground her teeth. "That is so not the point."

"Juniper Jones," Abby burst in. "A band Mom approves of. She even let me put their poster on my wall."

"It isn't the band, and you know it. It's the trip and the chaperones. And—" she glared at her daughter "—I've already made my decision."

Abby shook her head in patent disgust. She turned away, grabbed up a cup and drank.

"Hey, that's the Joker," Bobby said. "Give him back."

While the kids squabbled over the cup, Joe leaned toward Lisa. "I know it's pretty young for a trip across the state, but it's not like they're going alone."

"Her parents are part of the problem," Lisa hissed. "I have to worry about the lack of supervision. The Turners are irresponsible. Who knows what they'll allow? Besides the obvious danger of them losing my daughter."

"I'd bet whoever goes to the party will be considered the coolest kids in class. Whoever's parents treat them like babies, however…"

"I am not treating her like a baby."

"I doubt Abby sees it that way."

"Then this is one of those many times when she'll have to defer to my better judgment, like it or not. It isn't the first time, and I'm certain it won't be the last."

"What harm will it really do? Abby will stay with the group. She wouldn't smoke or drink, even if it were offered."

Lisa rubbed her neck. "You might understand this better if you were a father—"

Joe's expression blanked.

"But this is my decision, not hers. This choice will affect others I have to make later."

"I believe a person who hasn't biologically conceived could understand that," Joe said.

Lisa frowned at his stiff tone. "It isn't the conceiving that makes you a parent. It's the raising."

He cocked his head. "You don't think a person can learn to parent?"

"Of course. I'm still learning, every day."

Joe leaned back on his elbows and looked toward the rides, effectively distancing himself without moving. Lisa studied him for a moment, curious and a bit concerned over his brooding. She endured the silent treatment for a few minutes, then asked, "Do you want to go home?"

Bobby and Abby froze, then glanced at Joe, who took

longer to respond. He only shrugged. As the other three continued to stare, he sat up. "No, let's go have even more fun."

Lisa didn't care for his sarcasm, but the yips of relief from her kids cut off her protest. Still, she watched Joe for the rest of the afternoon. He behaved beautifully with her kids, but she sensed a remoteness. He didn't make eye contact with her, which was so unlike the Joe Riley she'd come to know, it unnerved her.

When they pulled into her driveway, she still hadn't succeeded in convincing him to stay for dinner in repayment for their day. Lisa told herself the let-down feeling in her belly stemmed from a full day of sunshine and too much pop.

But she wasn't fooled.

Joe carried in the cooler she'd insisted on packing for the ride home. They'd all been too full to need a drink, but she felt better for having tried to cut down on expenses.

"Sure I can't talk you into dinner?" Lisa smiled. "I was thinking of frozen pizza."

"I'd better be going."

"Oh." She glanced up the stairs. "Did I or the children do something to upset you?"

He jammed his hands in the pockets of his shorts. "No."

"Then what's wrong?"

"I've just been mulling over a problem."

She rolled her eyes. He always had work on his mind. "Okay, fine. Have it your way. Thanks for a nice day." She turned her back on his glare and called up the stairs, "Kids, come thank Mr. Riley."

They pounded down the steps.

"Thanks, Mr. Riley," Bobby said with a beaming smile. "It was the neatest day I ever had."

"Yeah, thanks." Abby hesitated, then stepped forward

and gave him a quick hug. She jumped away and ran up the steps with Bobby following.

Joe smiled, watching them go. "Maybe I could stay for dinner, after all."

She narrowed her eyes. "Or not."

He looked at Lisa. "What did I do now? You know, there's just no pleasing you." He blinked, then grinned. "Well, there is, but…"

"Don't start that again. I want to know what you're up to."

"What are you talking about?"

"A minute ago, you adamantly couldn't stay for dinner, now all of a sudden, after a smile from the kids, you're pulling up a chair and tucking in your napkin."

Joe looked around the living room. "I'm what?"

"Don't get smart. What's going on?"

"Nothing. I just want the kids to like me. Is that a crime? I thought you'd be happy."

"Why?" she asked.

"Don't you want your kids to like me?"

Lisa gave up. She led him to the kitchen, gave him instructions about washing his hands—which earned her a scowl worthy of Bobby—setting the table, and putting the pizza in the oven. "As long as you're here, you might as well help. I'll be back when the pizza's ready."

"Where are you going?"

"To take a shower."

Their gazes met. The gleam in his eyes made Lisa reconsider taking off her clothes with him in the house. She swallowed. Her pulse picked up and she shivered with need, imagining him in the shower with her. She wanted him too much. This couldn't be good for her. "Maybe I won't. You're a guest. I should make the—"

"Lisa." His knowing smile curled her toes. "Go on. I'll be right here. Thinking about you, and how you look, and aching, but go ahead."

"I think I will."

JOE THOUGHT his plan worked pretty well, except for a few tense moments over lunch. Bobby had hero worship in his eyes. Naturally Abby would be harder to convince. She shared a lot of her mother's stubbornness, but he'd win her over, too. Her hug convinced him he still had a chance.

It had made him catch his breath. Abby could be so endearing when she dropped the sulky attitude. He planned to work on Lisa about this concert thing. Poor Abby, who gave such heartwarming hugs, should get to go.

Joe cooked the pizza and tossed a salad, even managing some garlic butter on toasted bread as a surprise. The Meyer family showed their appreciation with hearty appetites. He didn't confess that doing things in the kitchen had kept him from going to do other things in the bathroom. With Lisa.

But he'd thought about it. Thought about it until he ached. Thought about it until he sweated. Thought about it until he'd been heading out of the kitchen when the oven timer buzzed.

"The Mustangs are the hardest team ever," Bobby said.

"Soccer," Lisa informed Joe.

"Ah." He nodded.

"Don't worry about it," Abby said. "They don't even keep score in kindergarten."

Bobby glowered. "We do, too."

"You're not supposed to."

"The coaches don't have to tell us who won," he said. "We know. And the Mustangs beated everybody they played."

"They beat everybody," Lisa corrected.

"Yeah, we're gonna get creamed." Bobby frowned and picked the pepperoni off his pizza, tossing it to the side of his plate.

Joe leaned toward Bobby. "Look, there's a simple way to win."

"There is?" Bobby's eyes gleamed.

"Simple?" Abby leaned toward them.

"It's not just about winning," Lisa said. "They're supposed to learn the rules of the game, play fair and have fun."

The three cast her pitying looks then huddled again.

"Those are all great things," Joe said, rolling his eyes for the kids' benefit and earning giggles, "but winning makes you feel good, and that's important, too."

"Joe," Lisa warned.

"I know, I know. Learn the rules, play fair and have fun. But you're supposed to improve, aren't you?" he asked Bobby. "Get better. Play smarter."

Bobby nodded. "Coach Martini says think about what you're doing."

"Exactly. Coach Martini wants you to play better. And in playing better, you'll also win more."

"That's not—" Lisa started.

"It's a natural outcome." He cut her off. "To play better, you need to research your opponent. Uh, watch the other team play, so you can find out their weaknesses and capitalize on them. You know, figure out who the bad players are and take the ball from them."

"There are no *bad* players," Lisa informed him.

Joe angled his body away from her. It was hard enough putting takeover strategy in kindergarten terms without having to be politically correct, as well.

"Of course, I don't mean bad in a negative way," he said

and ignored the scoff from Lisa. "I just mean the kids who aren't as fast, who don't kick as well, who have problems playing soccer."

"You mean, like me?" Bobby asked in a small voice, looking down at the table.

Joe cringed. *Aw, hell.* "No, of course not."

He stopped when Bobby glanced at him out of the corner of his eye. The boy had a point. Joe didn't know anything about Bobby's abilities or lack thereof. Not a setback, or, at least, not an insurmountable one. "What kind of player do you think you are?"

"Bobby tries very hard," his mother said.

"He doesn't totally stink," his sister said in support.

Bobby sat silently.

"Bob?" Joe leaned toward him.

"I'm not..." He swallowed. "I'm not very good."

Joe sat back. "Well, I don't know if that's true or not because I haven't seen you play. But whatever you do, don't let the other team know you think that way."

"Why not?"

"Because they'll see you as the kid they can take the ball away from."

Bobby grimaced. "They can."

"That's not important," Lisa said. "You always hustle and you're learning. You have fun and—"

"It *is* important," Joe overrode her. "If you go on the field thinking you're going to get creamed, you probably will. But if you go out there thinking, 'Hey, maybe I can dribble better than that boy,' or 'I might be able to score around that boy,' then you've got a better chance to do those things in the game."

"You think so?"

Joe nodded. "Attitude is everything. You've got to go out

on the field believing in yourself, even if you're not sure how well you play."

"But I already know I'm not good."

"Sometimes in life," Joe said, "you'll want something really badly that it seems like you can't have, and you're going to have to figure out how to get it. At those times, you can't think, 'I'm not good at this.' You have to find out how you're better and what your strengths are in each situation. Then use your strengths to get what you want."

"What if I don't have any strengths?"

Joe's chest burned. The kid's soulful eyes ate at him. "You have strengths, Bobby. Even without watching you play, I can say that because I've gotten to know you. You're smart, you're quick, and as I learned on my first visit to your house, you know how to kick."

They all laughed, Bobby's face turning red with a mixture of embarrassment, pride and humor.

"So, watch the other team," Joe said, "figure out who you're just as good as, and then go after him."

Bobby smiled and nodded. "I'll try."

Joe's chest swelled with the familiar sense of accomplishment. A short pep talk and the boy had renewed hope. Joe had a little new hope himself for his parenting skills.

"Joe Riley," Lisa said, "what are you doing with my children?"

Joe didn't need to glance at Lisa to see her expression. He could tell from her frosty tone.

He was in deep doo-doo.

Chapter Eight

Lisa crossed her arms over her chest and surveyed Joe. He was up to something, probably no good. Just when she'd been trusting him, almost. All right, not trusting him, but definitely softening toward him, and he had to ruin it.

Now she'd found him out. Sort of.

Of course, he was charm itself and could be as beguiling and as secretive as the devil she'd first thought him to be.

Lisa paused. When had she stopped thinking of Joe as the devil? This was bad. She couldn't get attached to him. He'd be gone soon. Gone, that was, as soon as she convinced his parents Joe could manage his own love life.

Okay, so he'd be around for longer than she'd anticipated because convincing the elder Rileys that Joe didn't need their help finding a wife would be nearly impossible. Eventually, Joe would either see through his mother's fragile-health act or become satisfied, enough time had passed for her to be treated as normal.

He appeared so innocent sitting there, as the children, wise to the nuances of their mother's voice as they were, scooted the heck out of Dodge. They edged along the wall, undoubtedly not wanting any stray fire ricocheting onto them. Lisa's heart swelled with pride to see the hesitation in their eyes, reading it as a sign of their loyalty to Joe, who had been trying to help Bobby. If only that had been his sole motive.

She just hoped she could uncover the rest of the plan lurking behind those gorgeous blue eyes. Why did the men in her life have to be deceitful? She should have known better with this one, who'd asked her to lie for him right after he introduced himself.

"What am I doing with them?" Joe repeated, obviously stalling. "What are you talking about?"

Lisa didn't know, exactly. Just her mother's intuition shooting off warning signals. She'd have to bluff and hope Joe didn't realize it.

She needed allies. She spotted the children still sidling along the wall, nearing the doorway to the kitchen.

"Sit down, kids." If the discussion got intense, she could always send them to their rooms.

Joe scowled.

Lisa glared.

Bobby fidgeted.

Abby smiled.

"What are you doing with my children?" Lisa said again.

His eyebrows came together in a frown as he spread his empty palms, making him appear innocent and baffled. "Eating dinner."

Bobby giggled. Abby had the sense to freeze.

"Don't get clever with me," Lisa warned in her parental tone, hoping it would bring Joe into line.

"If you could be more specific?" Joe said.

"This advice you're giving Bobby—"

"The boy needs a different approach," Joe cut in. "His basic attitude toward the game is defeatist. He'll never win that way."

Bobby hunched his shoulders and lowered his gaze.

"Sorry, Bob," Joe said before Lisa had a chance to reassure him. "I didn't mean you wouldn't be a winner, just that you and your team need to start thinking like winners before that can happen. Coach Martini will agree."

Lisa gave Joe credit for a quick recovery, thankful for his talent for deception this once, as her son's head rose and the glow came back into his eyes. It didn't negate the rest of Joe's faults, but she'd forgive him a lot for restoring her child's self-esteem.

She leaned back in her chair and recrossed her arms. "That doesn't explain your motivation."

"Making Bobby and his team better."

"And the ambitious light in your eyes?"

Joe ducked his head for a moment and came up with a sheepish grin. "I like to win."

The kids smiled at him. Lisa did not.

He shrugged. "I've spent my adult life trying to be the best in my field. After Dylan and I started up Riley and Ross, I spent my waking hours making it the best company in the electronics field." He shrugged again. "It's what I do."

"Don't you ever have fun?" Bobby asked with a frown.

"My work is my fun."

Lisa's breath caught in her throat. He said it so matter-of-factly. She didn't want him to live through his company. He should have something else. Her heart ached for him.

What would he have to retire to? For that matter, what did he have to come home to now? For some reason that idea disturbed Lisa more deeply than she could understand.

The children nodded, as if Joe getting "fun" from his work was just one more of those perfectly normal adult things they didn't understand.

"So when I see a situation like Bobby's," Joe said to the kids, "I just want to make it better. I want to be on the winning side. And, I'll admit, I thought Bobby needed a man's advice."

Lisa narrowed her eyes at him.

"He only wants us to like him, Mom," Bobby interrupted. He darted a glance at Joe, who behaved as though his shirt had suddenly shrunk on his body. "What's wrong with that?"

"Yeah," Abby challenged, "why can't he like us?"

She cocked an eyebrow at Joe.

The children glanced at their mother, then at Joe, then at her again. Their gazes came to rest on Joe, their eyes not as trustful, their expressions not as open.

Lisa hated to see them disillusioned. She needed to stop this conversation for their sake, but couldn't think of a way, short of sending the kids to their rooms, and it was too late for that now. She'd left it a moment too long. Or perhaps, she'd left it just long enough for Joe to hang himself.

"I'm really interested in your team, Bob."

As much as her heart ached for her children, Lisa felt sorrier for Joe, faced with the doubt on their faces. Since Brad had spent most of his time at the office, they'd never had a man interested in their activities. Having their mother support their efforts didn't come close to being enough.

Bobby nodded, never taking his gaze from Joe, as though Joe were an exotic beast just dropped into their dining room. Unknown and a little dangerous, but fascinating.

Then the eccentric man said, "When is your next game?"

"Next Saturday morning."

"Tell you what," Joe continued. "I usually put in a few hours at work on Saturdays, but I'd like to watch you play. Why don't I come to your game?"

The children's eyes grew wide. Bobby looked stunned, and Abby started laughing.

"You don't want to do that." Abby struggled for a serious expression. And lost. "You'd be…bored…to tears," she said between giggles.

Joe's mouth compressed.

"You don't have to come." Bobby scowled at his sister. "Not that it's boring—" he turned his earnest face back to Joe "—but you're really busy."

Lisa couldn't imagine what he was up to, but the idea of Joe at Bobby's soccer game? She couldn't picture it.

"What's wrong with me coming to the game, for Pete's sake?"

"It's hot," came immediately from Bobby.

"Or some days it's real cold," Abby added.

"It can be muddy," Bobby warned.

"And there's nothing to do," Abby assured him.

"Except watch me," Bobby tacked on with a hurt look.

"Yeah, but I'm your sister. I have to watch you."

Bobby nodded, placated.

Joe frowned. "Why don't you two want me to come?"

The kids lowered their gazes and looked as guilty as Lisa felt. Joe just didn't fit her idea of a sports parent. He was too consumed with business.

Then it hit her.

He needed to get out in the world, away from work, and her family was resisting his attempt. He'd never learn to play if they didn't help him. "You'd be more than welcome," she said. "It's Bobby's last soccer game of the season. Let me write down the game time for you."

JOE PULLED AT HIS TIE, trying to get more comfortable. He'd had trouble finding a parking spot at the park. Then he'd watched the wrong game for about ten minutes. Three other fields had games in progress, and he'd scoured the crowds at all three before he found Lisa.

Unlike him, she glowed in the sunshine rather than drooped. Khaki shorts showed off her legs. A tight, faded yellow tank top drew his attention to her other attributes, making the day seem even hotter. She'd tucked her blond hair under a baseball cap, giving her the overall picture of happy sports mom. She looked surprised to see him, which ticked him off, considering he'd said he would come.

Abby eyed him hesitantly, and then gave him a smile before she returned to an intense conversation with another girl. Lisa introduced him to Janet Something on the other side of her before she'd been pulled back into conversation.

The kids were right. It was hot and still muddy from the rainstorm the night before, which added to the humidity. He'd have to do a major cleanup on his deck shoes when he got back to the office. He eyed a guy's canvas folding chair with envy, especially the cup holder. He could sure use a cold drink himself. He pulled off his tie and shoved it in the pocket of his suit jacket.

"Are you Alice Riley's son?"

Joe turned to see a round, red-faced woman smiling up at him. He extended his hand. "Joe Riley."

She held his hand between both of hers. "Alice told us what a godsend you've been since her heart attack."

"Thank you, ma'am." He gave a little tug, to no avail.

"Mary Peters. Your mother and I play bridge together on Tuesdays. She's so relieved you're getting married."

Joe ground his teeth. Sweat layered his hand where she still clasped it.

"This is my husband, Charlie."

Charlie held out his hand, forcing Mary to relinquish Joe's. After shaking hands, the older man wiped his on his shorts.

"Hot day," Joe said, embarrassed.

"This is Alice and Mike Riley's boy, Joe. He's getting married this Christmas."

Joe groaned.

"Is your fiancée here?" Mary asked.

Crap. Joe pasted on a smile and tapped Lisa's arm.

She turned to him.

"Honey," he said, holding her gaze, "these are friends of my parents'."

Her eyes widened before she looked past him.

"Mary and Charlie Peters," he continued. "This is Lisa Meyer."

"We're so excited for you," Mary gushed. "I had a Christmas wedding, too."

Lisa stared at Joe. "Christmas?"

"Poinsettias."

She winced then turned to Mary. "We haven't actually set a date."

Janet Whoever stepped closer. "You're engaged?"

"No!" Lisa looked at Abby, who hadn't turned.

"But I'm sure Alice told me you are," Mary said.

Joe nodded then shook his head. "We're thinking about it."

"Please don't tell anyone," Lisa begged Janet. "We're just dating. I don't want to involve the kids until we're more sure."

"Of course not," Janet said. She gave Joe a once-over. "You can never be too careful."

He narrowed his eyes at her, and she stepped away.

Charlie wandered back to his chair. Mary remained, frowning. "You're not engaged?"

Joe glanced at Lisa.

"I'm dragging my feet." She smiled at the older woman. "You know how hard it is to train a man. I'm just not sure I'm ready for all that work."

Mary laughed. "You're so right, dear. Charlie and I have been married for forty-six years and I'm still breaking him in."

Lisa tossed Joe a cheeky smile and returned to her conversation with Janet as Mary went back to her seat.

Joe shook his head. Women.

He scanned the playing field and thought of the pile of work he'd left on his desk, at the time feeling pretty smug about coming. Now he wished himself back at the office, getting that work accomplished. Still, he couldn't shake the feeling attending this game would be an important step in discovering whether he was cut out for fatherhood.

He couldn't figure out which gold jersey belonged to Bobby. He needed to get the boy's attention so the kid would know he'd kept his promise, and then he'd be able to leave.

He leaned toward Lisa.

"The program has brought such changes to Ashley's vocabulary," Janet said in a self-satisfied tone. "I never thought to discuss the paintings of Degas with a second grader."

Joe rolled his eyes and tapped Lisa's arm.

She smiled at him, but Janet continued talking.

"But then, I should have known Ashley would take after me. I'm very interested in the arts. I even used to paint. I don't think you knew that, did you?"

"No, I—" Lisa said.

"I wasn't as talented as I would have liked," Janet said, "so I had to abandon it. But hopefully my son will build on the artistic genes I passed on to him and become the painter I could not be."

Joe wiped sweat off his forehead with a handkerchief. He removed his jacket and slung it over his arm.

"I'm sure Ashley will do you proud. He's already excelled in everything you've mentioned."

"Oh, yes…"

Joe gave up trying to get Lisa's attention. He scanned the field for Bobby. Some kids ran off the far side of the field and more ran onto it. Aha. Replacements. Sure enough, here came Bobby, throwing grass at a giggly little girl wearing an enormous gold bow to match her jersey.

Lisa still seemed engrossed in Janet's conversation about this arts program. The coolness of his office beckoned. He'd just wave to Bobby then leave. He needed to get back to his reports on profit margins and sales projections.

He picked out Bobby running down the field, kicking the ball—*too far in front of you, keep it closer*—when a girl in a green jersey barreled into Bobby. He fell to the ground, and the ball flew out of bounds.

Joe jerked as if he'd been hit with a Taser and forced himself not to run onto the field. The whistle blew, and Bobby's coach helped him to his feet. The boy rubbed at his bottom and nodded at the coach and the two referees, obviously choosing to stay in and play.

Joe's chest tightened with pride. *Atta boy. Hang tough.* He waited for the referee, a teenage boy, to line up a penalty for Bobby to kick. But he didn't. Play resumed with a green jersey throwing the ball in from the sideline. The ref hadn't even granted possession to Bobby's team.

A little irritated now at the two inept referees, Joe clenched his teeth and decided to stay a few minutes longer. Just then, the same girl ran into Bobby again. Bobby remained on his feet, but since he'd been nowhere near the ball, the referees hadn't seen it. No penalty. Joe seethed. That girl was running down Bobby on purpose.

Sure enough, Bobby got the ball a few minutes later, and the girl ran after him. She got closer. "Watch your back, Bobby," Joe called. "She's coming for you."

From the corner of his eye, he noticed Lisa twist his way but ignored her. If she hadn't been so intent on her conversation, she'd have seen those fouls. He couldn't explain now. Somebody had to watch out for her son.

"Come on, come on," he muttered. Bobby put on a burst of speed but ran past the ball. Joe groaned. The little girl in the green jersey stayed on Bobby's heels.

Just then Bobby fell.

Joe had had it. "Hey, Ref, how about a foul call here? That girl is knocking our player all over the place."

"Joe." Lisa grabbed his forearm, trying to hush him. She couldn't believe him, yelling like this. He'd said he was ambitious and liked to win, but hollering at the two kids refereeing the game?

"What?" He glanced at her then back to the field. In a loud voice, he called, "Hey, Ref, give us a break."

Abby turned around with wide eyes, then ducked her head. One hand came up to cover the side of her face.

"Joe," Lisa hissed again, with a tug on his arm.

"What?"

"Would you lower your voice?"

"The refs won't hear me if I do that."

"And neither will the other parents."

When he looked at her as though he didn't understand her language, Lisa knew she'd better act quickly. "Those kids are all trying their best to learn the game."

"Well, that one little girl—" he jabbed a pointed finger toward the field to indicate Miranda Destin "—is learning guerilla tactics. She's pushing Bobby down on purpose."

Lisa flushed when Bill Destin swiveled in his chair to glare at Joe. She forced a smile and nodded. "Bill."

He nodded but didn't return her smile. He squinted a warning glance at Joe before pointedly turning his back to them both.

"Listen," she said, keeping one eye on Bill, "the kids are learning soccer from the coaches, but they're also learning from the parents."

"Learning what?" Joe glared at Bill. "Bullying?"

Bill's back stiffened.

Lisa pinched Joe's arm under his jacket so no one would see her. Having gained his full attention, she held his gaze with hers. "Behave."

Joe scowled.

"That's what the players are learning right now—you being a bully to the refs, and I'd appreciate it if you showed them good sportsmanship. You and I both know that some kids elbow others and push them deliberately." She got in her own dig at Miranda's continuous pursuit of Bobby. Bill appeared rooted in his chair. Still, that kind of retaliation wouldn't teach Joe anything. "But the important thing for Bobby is how he handles it."

Joe inhaled a deep breath and let it out in a prolonged sigh. A pretty graceful concession. Her heart swelled at his attempt to defend her child. The reasons she'd asked him to come to the game returned to her now. He needed to learn to relax. Winning felt good, but it didn't keep a person warm at night. She wanted to be the one to teach Joe these things.

She had special insight into the matter, after all. Her husband, who'd put work first, had never gotten to know his children. Maybe the time had come to tell Joe about Brad, and all the things he'd missed out on that she didn't want Joe to sacrifice.

"Come over later," she said. A wary look crossed his face. His arm tensed under her hand. She could almost see him forming excuses to go back to work, to a world he knew. Back to a place that isolated him. "Bobby will need reassurance," she said, not above using his fondness for her son.

Still he hesitated.

"I'll let you sample some of my goodies."

He slid her a dubious glance.

She grinned. "I made cookies."

LISA LEANED BACK against the counter, preparing the words she wanted to say to Joe.

How could she explain about Brad? She had brooded over him for months, trying to figure out what had motivated him to work so much. But the truth lay in her ex-husband's nature. As a workaholic, he felt compelled to succeed, to the point his family came not only second place but even farther down the list.

She envisioned Joe heading in the same direction.

Lisa sighed, not sure if she could save him, but knowing she had to try. Her heart ached, thinking of Joe living his life alone. Although he might marry someday, that didn't ensure he'd be any less alone than most workaholics.

The idea of Joe with a wife soured her stomach. Although she could never marry another man as ambitious as her ex, she was honest enough to admit she'd fantasized about a fling with Joe. Heck, if she didn't have to worry about the children, she'd fling herself right at him.

The more time she spent with him, the more she liked him. Although he'd asked her to lie, he'd done it so he wouldn't have to hurt his mother. Although he worked too much, he'd built a company to be proud of, employed dozens of locals and put their tiny town of Howard on the lips of people in the electronics world, as well as in print in business magazines. Although he was handsome as the devil, he spent time with her children instead of chasing women.

She couldn't bring herself to have an affair with him, but she cared enough to help Joe see where his career path led. To a lonely existence.

The sounds of the children going to their rooms yanked Lisa back to the problem at hand. She lifted the plate of cookies and headed into the living room.

Joe smiled. "I thought you'd forgotten me."

Right. As if she could forget him.

"I want to talk to you." Lisa set the cookies on the end table at his elbow.

That didn't sound promising, Joe thought.

"Thanks for saying such encouraging things to Bobby about his playing. He looks up to you, you know."

Joe took a cookie and bit into it. Knowing full well Lisa's desserts tasted like heaven, he realized the extent of his dread when the cookie scraped down his throat like sandpaper.

Wanting to talk. Giving him cookies. Paying him compliments. Reminded of the Trojan horse, Joe wanted to flee. His instincts screamed at him, *Get out of here.*

She was rejecting his advances. She wanted to break off their arrangement. She intended to tell his mother the truth.

Joe swallowed the treat with a dry gulp. "I'd love to stay, but I have to run." Yeah, that sounded manly. "I mean, I have something else to do." Not wanting her to think he had to meet a woman, he added, "Work."

For some reason, the lines tightened around her mouth. He stared, tempted to ease her frown away with his lips, to give her something pleasant to think about, to feel her breath on his cheek.

She was talking.

Too late to flee.

"What? I'm sorry, I wasn't listening." Great. That'd get him nowhere with her. "I was thinking of…a problem at the office."

"That's what I want to talk to you about."

"My work problem?" Somehow he'd really missed the conversation here. He didn't have a problem at work, but he figured he could think up one if it kept her from that serious talk she looked determined to have.

"Your work problem," she repeated. "That's a very good way to phrase it."

He nodded, having no clue what she meant.

"Brad had a work problem, too."

"Your husband?"

"My ex, if you don't mind."

He didn't mind. In point of fact, he was mighty pleased the idiot had left the way clear for him.

"Brad's problem was the same as yours. He worked all the time, right from the moment we returned from our very brief honeymoon, if you could call it that. We only went away for the night to a local hotel. Then we came home and lived with his parents for a year, until they moved."

"Couldn't stand being around the newlyweds, huh?" Joe joked, not really wanting to think of her with another man, even a young husband.

"They couldn't stand being around the baby."

"Baby?" He glanced at the steps leading to the kids' rooms. "Abby?"

"I was pregnant when we got married." She shrugged. "I thank God I have a wonderful child like Abby and was blessed again with Bobby, but the timing could have been better."

He nodded. "Is that why your husband worked so hard to provide for your family?"

She raised her eyebrows.

"I'm not taking his side, but I do understand the male need to provide. The pressure and the joy of working."

"Who do you provide for, Joe?"

"What?" The question threw him. Her eyes bored into him, pinning him in place. He fidgeted under her regard.

"I'm talking about your lonely future. You staying later and later at work, trying to build something out of nothing. Trying to get a better position, make more money. I'm talking about you not knowing your children."

"You're talking about him, not me." He clenched his teeth. "I own the company I work for, so getting a better position doesn't apply. I don't have a wife or children."

"Maybe it's not you now," she said, "but I'm afraid it could be. This is why your mother wants you to have something else, too, something to save you from becoming like Brad. She believes a wife is the answer."

Lisa laughed, a harsh, humorless sound. "I know from firsthand experience that a wife or even children may not be enough. Brad had me and the kids, but did it save him from working himself to numbness? Did it save him from coming home late, night after night, too tired to eat or talk or sleep or…anything?"

The words hung in the air, as clearly as if she'd said them. He wondered how long it had been since Lisa and her husband had made love before he'd left her. If Joe weren't so pissed off, he'd work on rectifying that mistake. But she'd practically accused him of abandoning his future family, and he was damned if he'd pay for Brad's sins.

"Do you see what I'm saying?"

"Oh, I see it all right."

"I'm worried about you. I don't want you to take the same path he did. I don't want work to be the only joy you have." She glanced at her laced fingers. "I care about you, Joe. I don't want you to end up like him, alone and unhappy." She grimaced. "Well, maybe not alone, but you get my point."

"I get your point," he said gruffly.

Lisa jerked back, surprise clear on her face.

"Now you get mine." He surged to his feet, too agitated to sit still. He towered over her armchair, but mad as he was, he didn't want to frighten her. Stepping away, he cleared his throat and forced himself to keep his voice low, not wanting to alarm the children, either. All he needed was to get into a loud argument with Lisa, upsetting the kids.

"Listen," he said with great control, "and listen good. Point one. I would not take off with some young girl. That's your husband, not me. Try not to confuse us."

He paced away, then turned on his heel to face her. "Point two. I would never, I repeat, *never* walk away from my children. I wouldn't walk away from my wife, for that matter, not without trying to make our marriage work. Not without damned good cause.

"Marriage is sacred. I have the example of my own parents to guide me. Believe me, when the time is right, I'll make that step, but it'll take the right woman to convince me. I've got to know she's worth giving up everything for."

He couldn't believe he'd just said that. What did he think he'd be giving up, his wonderful bachelor existence?

Determined not to be sidetracked, he reminded himself where he'd been going with that thought. His parents. "My mom wants me to find someone, sure, but not just because I work too much, although I'll admit she thinks so. Mom missed me while I was living in California. Now that I'm back in the same town, she's eager for the grandma thing. My dad, too."

Joe winced inwardly, remembering his dad's advice about having a family and being home for the kids. *Not now, Dad.* Words of wisdom could plague him later. He had to stay focused. He wouldn't take the fallout for her ex-husband's mistakes.

He was jealous as hell of the guy.

Not that it made sense, but when in his relationship with Lisa had sense entered into anything? He took a breath and stepped toward her.

"Maybe your husband enjoyed what he was doing. Don't you think he got a sense of accomplishment from it he couldn't find anywhere else? No offense, but changing diapers doesn't fill any deep-seated need for guys any more than it thrills women."

"But he wasn't around for that. He was working—"

"You say it as though working is the worst thing in the world."

Lisa's mouth firmed. "It isn't the worst thing, Joe, but

it became an obsession for him. I don't want that to happen to you."

Joe couldn't believe she was comparing him to that loser. Jealousy and anger mixed into a lethal combination. "Are you sure he loved his work as much as you claim?"

"Brad worked all hours, staying late, sometimes going in on Saturdays, just as you do. I tried to make our home as welcoming and relaxing as possible, but he just wanted to be at the office. I don't want that to happen to you."

His resentment sparked. "Did it ever occur to you maybe your ex came home late and was gone on weekends, not because he'd been working, but because he'd been having affairs all along?"

Chapter Nine

Lisa blanched white, and Joe reached out a hand to steady her in her chair. He went cold himself as he realized what he'd done. How could he have hurt Lisa? "I'm sorry."

She shook her head, face averted.

"Lisa, I'm so sorry. I didn't mean—" He stopped himself because he believed it. "I didn't mean to hurt you."

That, at least, was the truth, although a lot of good it did now.

She put a hand over her face.

Joe would have done anything to take the words back. He knelt by her chair. "Can I get you something? A drink? Water?"

"No." Her voice came out croaky, but at least she was still talking to him.

He balled his hand into a fist, wanting to shove it into a wall. Idiot. His jealousy had run away with his brain, and all he could think of was defending himself.

"You're right," Lisa said with her hand still over her eyes. "I've been stupid."

"No, no, of course not. I'm sure he covered up his activities. You couldn't have guessed." His chest burned. Yearning to make her feel better, he said, "Maybe I'm wrong."

She shook her head violently.

"All this time, it was right there." She raised her gaze to Joe, but he doubted she'd focused outside her memories. "I didn't see it. I never knew."

He took her hand. "Guys like him conceal things. You weren't supposed to know."

Finally her gaze centered on him. The anguish in the lovely blue depths pierced him.

"I'm sorry," she said, "but I'd like you to go now."

The blood left his head, leaving behind a chill clamminess.

"I just need to be alone," she added.

"No," he protested, squeezing her hand to keep her with him. He had to do…something. If only she would stay here with him, he'd think of the right answer. He'd hold her in his arms until she felt better. Whatever she needed, he wanted to provide it.

"Joe, please."

He found himself incapable of argument. How could he insist she take comfort from him when he'd caused her pain?

"I'll be fine," she said.

Joe studied her expression, which she kept blank. It didn't convince him, but he couldn't very well force his company on her. With a heavy heart, he walked to the door.

"Call me. If you want to talk or if you need anything. I don't care what time it might be. Don't worry about waking me up."

As though he'd sleep.

She nodded and closed the door behind him.

He knew she wouldn't call, not if hell itself froze over.

LISA LAY IN BED the next morning, still queasy from thoughts of Brad cheating throughout their marriage. Her brain felt muddled and fuzzy from her sleepless night, most of it spent crying. At least she hadn't started sobbing until after Joe left.

She groaned and buried her head in her pillow where she'd stifled her tears.

As his words sank in, her face had gone cold and numb, certainly draining of color. Judging by the concern on his face, she must have appeared close to passing out. She'd never fainted in her life—when would she have had time? She'd ushered Joe out the door, nearly slamming it on his heels. His repeated apologies still sounded in her ears.

Humiliated didn't begin to describe how clueless she felt. Had everyone in town known except her? Although only supposition, Joe's words held the ring of truth. Thinking back on her years with Brad, Lisa could pick out events now, which should have sent up giant red flags at the time. Maybe she hadn't wanted to believe what she knew in her heart.

How could she have lived with Brad if she acknowledged his unfaithfulness? Going through the divorce had been traumatic for her and the kids. Perhaps not seeing the problem had been her way of avoiding the inevitable. Forgiving Brad and working with a counselor on their problems would never have been an option, not even for the sake of the children. Once lost, her trust would never be regained.

She groaned again, but this time forced herself out of bed. The world wouldn't stop just because she felt lousy. She planned to attend the special Memorial Day Sunday service today. A glance at the clock assured her the family still had enough time to make it if she got Abby and Bobby moving. She could definitely use some calm reflection time. Church, with its quiet peace, would provide the proper atmosphere for starting to heal.

JOE CHECKED his watch again, then looked toward Lisa's front door. She didn't answer, and it was now past noon.

He'd waited until the discount store opened for Sunday business, then bought a present for the kids. The idea came to him as he lay in bed, wide-awake, around four that morning. He'd arrived at the Meyer house at ten-thirty to find no one home. At first, he'd wondered if Lisa just wasn't answering, but a peek through the side window of her garage showed her van missing.

He tossed the basketball at the portable hoop he'd set up for Bobby and Abby on Lisa's driveway. The ball ricocheted wide, and he trotted over to snatch it out of the neighbor's flower border. Not too crushed, he thought. Unlike Lisa.

He was such a moron. He smacked the ball on his forehead, berating himself for blurting out his suspicions about her ex. Stupid, stupid, stupid.

The truth had shone in her eyes. Somewhere inside, she'd known about her ex-husband's infidelity. She'd just been denying the evidence living with him provided. A previously effective defense mechanism, which Joe had demolished with a few careless words.

Now he understood her strong independent streak. She'd sheltered herself with a cloak of pride for so many years, relied on it when she couldn't count on anyone else in her life.

With a pang in his chest, he realized he wanted to be the one she relied on. Not knowing where that path would lead scared him a little. If he had any sense of self-preservation, he'd get out of here before they arrived. But he couldn't erase the image of Lisa's face draining of color. She'd lost her illusions, and Joe had been the one who'd ripped away the veil.

When their dark green minivan pulled into the driveway, he smiled and gave a brief wave. Would Lisa welcome him? Should he give her more time to come to terms with his accusations?

Shaking his head, Joe knew he wouldn't leave her alone. He had to see her and give her whatever support she would accept from him. At the very least, he could keep the kids busy shooting hoops so Lisa could have time to herself.

"Mr. Riley," Bobby called the minute his door opened. "Is that for us?"

Lisa climbed from the van, her pale peach sundress adding a warm glow to her skin. The skirt swirled around her legs, drawing his attention. The heat hadn't affected her as it had him. Sweat dripped down his back, while she appeared cool and softly feminine. Even the polish on her toenails piqued his interest.

Not that he had a chance with her now, after his asinine behavior the night before.

Joe avoided making eye contact with her. He had experienced her opinion on his giving gifts to her kids. Clearing his throat and pasting on a smile, he nodded.

Bobby's glee resounded through the neighborhood. Even Abby smiled as she shut her door. Then they turned to look at their mother.

Lisa's glare at Joe spoke all the thoughts she didn't voice. The kids' presence saved him from a tongue-lashing.

"What do you think, Mom?" Bobby asked.

"Be sure to say thank-you," she replied, her jaw tense.

Abby's mouth dropped open. "We can keep it? Really?"

Lisa met her daughter's eyes. "That doesn't mean you aren't in trouble for the remarks in the car, young lady. But, yes, you can keep the basketball hoop."

"Thank you, thank you!" Bobby yelled. He ran over and

grabbed the ball from Joe's hands. Then as he studied the basket, his face fell.

Joe grasped the situation immediately. "It adjusts."

He unscrewed the bolt on the back support, which he'd left loose enough to turn by hand for just this reason. After lowering the upper brace to accommodate the kids' heights, he fit it back together. "I'll just be a minute. Don't shoot until it's ready."

"I won't," Bobby vowed.

Joe picked up the crescent wrench and tightened the support. He turned to Lisa, who stood with her arms crossed, watching him. "It's a simple adjustment."

When she didn't answer, he added, "The whole thing rolls, so you can move it out of the way. It's light enough Abby and Bobby could move it when they're done playing each day, if they work together."

"Change out of your church clothes," she told the kids, who scampered off.

Lucky, Joe thought, watching them escape. He braved her censure alone. "I wanted to do something for them."

She stiffened, her lips thinning. "You don't need to feel sorry for them, Joe."

"It's not pity," he cut in. "I just thought this was something I could do that you wouldn't have the physical strength for."

Something you'd need a man for. Joe shook his head at himself. He wanted her to need *him.*

He recalled Lisa's words to her daughter. Maybe he could offer her a sounding board. "What's going on with Abby?"

Lisa ran a hand into her hair and growled. "That girl. She's still on me about the concert with Sally Turner."

"Tell me again why this birthday party is such a bad idea."

She glared at him through her sunglasses. "Don't you start in on me, too. I've been over it with her all morning. The Turners are lax in their discipline. I've met them several times, and I haven't been impressed."

She shook her head. "They're letting a nine-year-old have a birthday party where the guests have to be transported across the state, to stay overnight in another city. If that isn't bad enough, which it is, they're too indulgent. I watched Sally in church this morning."

Ah. Now he understood where the latest outburst originated. "They go to your church?"

"No, Sally attended with another friend. She danced during hymns and made faces during the sermon."

"That's natural for a kid, isn't it?"

"But not appropriate. By the time a child turns nine, she should understand what's acceptable. Even Bobby, at six, knows better."

Joe grinned. "But then, he has you for a mother."

"Exactly. If the Turners were good parents, they would have taught Sally better. Besides, she's been to school assemblies. She knows what's expected."

"How did Sally's behavior get Abby in trouble?" A bead of sweat trailed down Lisa's collarbone, distracting him.

"She started mimicking Sally, for starters. It worries me, the influence Sally has on Abby. Usually Abby thinks for herself. Lately, all she can think about is being like Sally."

"That's understandable, certainly?" The bead slid between her breasts. Joe swallowed and yanked his attention back to her face.

"Of course." Lisa threw her hands in the air. "It just isn't a good thing. I need to know Abby can withstand peer pressure. With Sally, I'm not sure she can."

"So talk to her."

Lisa slanted him a look. "What an excellent idea."

Joe winced. "Sorry. Of course you've tried. It's not working?"

"To put it mildly."

He thought for a moment. She'd said "for starters" when referring to Abby. "Okay, so what else did Abby do to get in trouble?"

"She's got a smart mouth."

Joe laughed. "Gee, I never would have believed it. She's always so nice to me."

"You know what I mean. She's sassing me."

He sobered. "Oh. That doesn't sound like Abby."

"Exactly my point. She's learning bad habits. Not using her head. Letting Sally cloud her judgment."

"Maybe…" He trailed off, sensing dangerous waters.

"Maybe what?"

Yep, Lisa had her shark face on.

"Maybe she's just being eight and a half. Maybe Abby would be trying out her wings without Sally's influence."

"Of course she would. She's testing herself, the boundaries, and me. I get that."

He wanted to side with Abby. A simple birthday party going to see a band Lisa approved of shouldn't be such a traumatic decision to make. Sure, the concert was across the state, but Abby had common sense enough to stay with the adults, wouldn't talk to strangers or go off alone. Didn't all girls go in herds to the bathroom, anyway?

Sometimes nothing a person said could make things better. He'd just be available, to listen, to provide a shoulder to lean on, to care. Joe stepped closer and took her hand.

Lisa started but didn't pull away.

"I'm sorry," he said. "It must be hard."

Her face softened. "We've always been so close."

"Growing pains?"

She sighed. "For both of us."

"Let me take you out to lunch. All of you." Joe smiled then locked his gaze on hers. "I owe you."

"For all those wonderful dinners?" she said in a breezy tone.

"No," he said, fully aware she meant to avoid the subject, "for the pain I caused you last night."

She looked away. "I don't want to talk about it."

He wanted to apologize, but she didn't seem receptive. "It's a holiday weekend, so let's go out. It'll look good for all my mom's friends, who can report back to her. Besides, I'm going out of town on Tuesday, and I'll be gone a week."

"Oh."

"It's business. I'm interviewing an engineer and a programmer, plus I'm meeting with a company whose business Dylan and I want to cultivate."

"You don't have to explain anything to me."

"I feel like I should." He smiled. "You're my fiancée after all."

Lisa laughed.

"I'll miss you." Joe stepped forward and put his arms around her, waiting for her to reject his move. When she didn't, he hugged her closer. His mouth brushed her lips tentatively, testing her response.

Lisa kissed him back. Too relieved to push it, he kept the kiss light. More than friendly, but less than passionate.

When she didn't pull away, he couldn't believe his luck. She'd forgiven him.

They let the kids shoot some hoops before they left. Lisa took the opportunity to change into more casual clothes while Joe "showed the kids some moves." Glancing out her bedroom window, she held back her giggles with a hand over her mouth, even though they wouldn't hear her with the sash closed against the heat. No doubt he was doing his Globetrotter imitation to amuse the children so she could have a moment alone.

She needed it after his announcement. Leaving town on business. Brad's version of business or legitimate meetings? She had no right to expect Joe to be faithful. Their agreement gave her no hold on him. That she wanted one surprised her. When had she become possessive of Joe?

Without an audience, she could appreciate the natural athleticism of his body. His Kansas City Chiefs T-shirt clung to his body in sweaty patches she should have found repulsive. The way the man could move turned her on, which unsettled her. It's a pretense, she reminded herself. She needed to reconcile her feelings toward Brad and his infidelity before she could start a relationship with another man.

Joe had been right the previous evening. She'd taken out her anger at Brad on Joe. They did have many faults in common, faults which made her leery of trusting Joe. Dishonesty, evasiveness, creative storytelling—and not in a Hans Christian Andersen kind of way.

But when she considered it, Joe hadn't really done anything else wrong. He hadn't betrayed her trust. He'd explained why he needed to fool his mother into thinking he was off the market, and his reasons had been to protect Alice and her "fragile" health.

Lisa frowned. She hadn't gotten to the bottom of that pretense, either. Yet she felt certain, almost certain anyway, Alice Riley could outact Meryl Streep. Women's intuition had her doubting Alice needed the coddling Joe bestowed on her. However misguided his solution, Lisa couldn't fault him for caring.

Although if he hadn't come up with his charade, they wouldn't have met as they had. A shiver ran over her skin, and Lisa thought she must be too close to the air-conditioning vent.

If they had been introduced at the Garden Society event, with her catering and Joe there to show support for his mom, what would have happened? If she'd had a moment to breathe during her duties, she would have thought him attractive, certainly, but would she have been open to a relationship? Lisa thought not. She'd been so focused on reducing her debt and holding on to her anger against Brad, she hadn't contemplated having a man in her life.

Now, for however brief a period, she had Joe.

She ran down the stairs, barely noticing the steps beneath her feet. The four of them bundled into her van, Joe's blue sportster not large enough to accommodate them, and headed for lunch.

They went to a family restaurant nearby, which had a twenty-minute wait but offered food appealing to the kids as well as the two adults. Lisa grit her teeth into a smile every time Joe put his arm around her waist and turned her toward yet another of his parents' acquaintances. By the time their table became available, she felt she'd met every senior citizen in Missouri and half of Kansas.

She recognized a few of their names from living in Howard all her life and hoped none of them kept in touch with her mom in Arizona. She made a mental note to call her mother and offer some kind of warning. Her mom would no doubt find the escapade hilarious.

"So," Joe asked after he finished eating, "what do you kids want to do now?"

"Now?" Lisa echoed.

"You don't have plans, do you?" He grimaced. "Sorry, I should have asked you first. I'm new at this."

She shook her head, resigned. She'd agreed to play his loving, almost fiancée in public. Obviously buoyed by the reception at the restaurant, Joe must want to capitalize on it before leaving town.

"I like putt-putt," Bobby said.

"It's like golf," Abby told Joe earnestly, "but with little windmills and tricky shots."

Joe bit his lip and nodded just as seriously. Lisa could have kissed him.

"Putt-putt it is," he said.

When they got to the parking lot, however, the sky had clouded over. So did the kids' faces.

"What do you think?" Joe asked Lisa, eyeing the sky.

"We'll never get through a game."

Abby's shoulders drooped. Bobby's mouth firmed, scowl in place. Great, Lisa thought, expecting a meltdown.

Joe laid a hand on the boy's shoulder. "Any good movies on?"

Bobby blinked and took a deep breath, then let it out in a gust. The change from petulant to eager boy stemmed more from Joe's touch than his suggestion.

"There are a couple things I'd like to see," Abby said in a small voice, wide eyes on Joe. "But I don't know what time they start."

Joe smiled at her. "Let's go find out."

Lisa drove to the cinema complex, mulling things over. The kids both responded to Joe. Was that a good thing?

With the start of summer looming, quite a few kids' movies had opened the previous Friday. Abby and Bobby agreed on one beginning in half an hour. Lisa wondered how Joe would do sitting through an animated feature.

He bought the tickets and returned with a grin. "This should be good. I love cartoons."

Lisa shook her head. She should have known.

Once again, every eye in the place watched as Joe ushered her into the theater. Lisa had never felt so awkward. She expected to trip over her feet with nerves at any second. She barely got to her seat when a thin, gray-haired woman did a double take, then nearly bent over staring at them. Lisa caught Joe's eye as the woman approached.

"I thought I recognized you," she said, eyes on him.

Joe stood. "I'm sorry. I have a terrible memory. When did we meet?"

"We haven't met actually. I've just seen your picture so many times at Alice's, I'd know you anywhere. I'm Susan Bennington."

Joe introduced Lisa and the kids.

"Oh, aren't you precious?" Susan said to Abby and Bobby, not noticing their grimaces. "Alice is so excited to get a jump start on grandchildren."

Bobby glanced around the semi-lit room, not paying attention to the adult conversation, but Abby narrowed her eyes at the woman, a murderous gleam peeking through.

"She's thrilled about having a daughter, too," Susan assured Lisa.

"I'm so glad," Lisa said, trying to catch her own daughter's eye.

Abby's expression turned stormy. Her pale skin flushed a deep pink, and her lips thinned. The muscles in her jaw ticked as she clenched her teeth. "Mom."

"Don't interrupt, dear," Lisa said to forestall her.

"But, Mom, this woman thinks—"

"Abigail, I said don't interrupt."

Her tone got through to the girl, who crossed her arms over her chest and glowered.

Joe turned on the charm, distracting Susan from any possible thoughts of discord among his future family. She left, happily unaware of the pending outburst.

"Mom, what did that woman mean?" Abby asked.

"Excuse us," Lisa said to Joe. "Would you mind watching Bobby while we, um, use the ladies' room?"

"No problem." Joe met her gaze, alert to the problem. She shook her head, indicating she didn't need his help with this. She hoped she was right.

Lisa escorted Abby out to the lobby. "First off, don't plan on getting your way by having a public temper tantrum. Secondly, since you usually don't have them, I'll let it go this time. Besides, I agree you have a right to an answer."

"If we're someone's grandkids other than Grammy and Gramps and Grandma Gen, you'd have to get married."

"Mrs. Bennington misunderstood. Well, the person she got the information from did. At least, she doesn't have the right idea." Lisa rubbed at her temple, frustrated with the web of lies. "Let me try this again. I'm not marrying anyone. Does that help?"

"Oh." Abby nodded. After a moment where Lisa could almost see the cogs connecting in her brain, Abby said, "Then why did that lady think you are?"

"Long, complicated story. Let's just say I don't have any plans to marry. I might date Mr. Riley, though. You need to be prepared for that. So his parents and other people they know might think that means we're getting married, but we aren't. Okay?"

She pushed a length of Abby's fine blond hair behind her ear. The girl nodded, a contemplative expression still on her face. "I know you and Dad aren't getting married again."

Although put forth as a statement, the question lingered. "No, honey," Lisa said gently, "we're not."

Abby nodded. "Sometimes Bobby thinks so, but I don't. Lots of my friends' parents are divorced, too. I know it means forever, and that's okay with me 'cause Dad just left us."

Lisa waited. She'd have other opportunities to talk about Brad's defection and help Abby work through her anger. For now, she'd listen and let Abby get whatever bothered her off her chest.

"So you're not going to marry Mr. Riley."

Again, a question echoed behind the statement.

"No," Lisa assured her, wondering if her kids would ever be ready for her to take that step. "We're just dating. It's nice to be with other grown-ups, to talk about things and just generally hang out." Lisa smiled as she borrowed Abby's phrase for every activity involving friends.

These days Lisa's only friend was Ginger, but she vaguely recalled those earlier years, before she got pregnant and married, when groups of her girlfriends went everywhere together. She really needed to get out more now the children were older.

"But you might?" Abby asked.

"Might what?"

"Marry Mr. Riley."

The impact of the question hit Lisa's chest and reverberated down to her stomach. "No."

"Isn't that why people date? To see if they like each other good enough to get married?"

"Well enough," Lisa corrected automatically. "And yes, that's one reason, but not in this case. We're just having fun together."

"I wouldn't mind."

"If I dated? Thanks, hon."

"No. I mean, no, I don't care about that. I like Mr. Riley. But I mean I wouldn't care if you married him."

Certain her smile wobbled as her knees did at the idea, Lisa led Abby back to their seats.

THE WEEK JOE STAYED in California stretched agonizingly long for Lisa. She didn't normally see him on a day-to-day basis and didn't understand why his absence on a business trip affected her so strongly. She couldn't concentrate and found little joy in the preparations she had to finish for her current commission.

She called Ginger, but even her friend couldn't offer a distraction. After talking for a few minutes, Ginger said she had other obligations and promised to call back. Hanging up, Lisa wondered if Ginger's reluctance to chat had to do with the Baby Project not going well.

School ended without Bobby getting into any fights. Having the kids underfoot only added to Lisa's frazzled nerves. Abby grew more despondent with the approach of Sally's party. Two girls from her class called every day to update Abby on the plans, making her more determined to change her mother's mind. Lisa hated to see Abby's sulky, accusatory face, but she didn't alter her answer. Eventually, Sally invited someone else to use the purchased ticket.

The tension in the house upset Bobby. His temper flared at unexpected times, reinforcing Lisa's determination to keep a hold on hers. Surprisingly, Bobby came up with his own solution when he got mad. He'd go outside and shoot baskets. Lisa frequently thought she should take a few shots herself.

Joe returned Sunday, the evening of the concert.

"Hi," Lisa said, feeling awkward. She wanted to grab him and hold on tight.

Joe held his arms out to his sides and grinned. "No presents, even though I wanted to. I learned my lesson."

She smiled.

"Hi, Mr. Riley," Bobby said. "You want to play basketball with me?"

After a glance at Lisa, Joe said, "Sure."

Abby stayed in her room, plugged in to her Juniper Jones CD.

Joe distracted Bobby with endless games of Horse, played under the security light on the garage. Joe had to copy Bobby's technique and stand where Bobby shot the ball. Often, Bobby turned his back to the net and tossed it over his shoulder. Lisa had seen him practice the shot all week, and she loved to hear Bobby's laugh when Joe had to try the same move. She suspected Joe often missed on purpose and let Bobby show off his newfound expertise with the basketball, and she blessed Joe for his sensitivity. She enjoyed having him "home," which rather freaked her out.

Monday rolled around, and Lisa answered a knock on the door around midmorning, surprised to see Joe on her porch. She led him into the kitchen where she had pork steaks marinating in Italian salad dressing.

"Don't you have to go to work?" she asked him.

He stretched with a yawn, his white oxford shirt molding to his chest muscles. Lisa smiled to herself, enjoying the view.

"I went in early so I could give everything to my secretary to type up. I've already briefed Dylan on how things went. So for the rest of the day, I'm all yours."

The pictures her imagination provided made her mouth go dry. His gaze met hers, and a slow smile spread across his face.

"Well, now," Joe said, either reading her mind or noticing the yearning in her expression. He leaned across the table and placed his lips to hers. The brief brush held promise.

Abby stomped into the foyer, causing them to break apart. She glared. "Oh, it's you."

Lisa bit her tongue, forcing herself not to rebuke her daughter. Abby had been quiet or angry in turns all weekend, but this morning she showed less control over her emotions, appearing close to tears.

"Hello, Abby," Joe said.

"Hi." She set her chin.

"Would you like something to drink?" Lisa asked.

"They haven't called me yet," Abby cried, eyes boring into her. "It's all your fault. Nobody likes me anymore because I couldn't go to the party. They think I'm a baby."

She ran from the room. The door to her room slammed on her sobs.

"Shouldn't you do something?" Joe asked, glancing up the stairs.

Lisa shook her head and walked into the kitchen. She refilled a glass of water and drank most it. "She'll have to be mad at me for a while. Don't worry, I can take it."

"Can you?" Joe stepped to her side and put his arm around her waist.

She stiffened, knowing she'd break down if she went into his embrace. He tugged, and she folded into him, seeking his support. He stroked her hair as she struggled not to cry.

"It'll be all right," he whispered.

"I know."

"She'll forgive you."

"I know." Still, Lisa burrowed in closer.

He just held her, rocking gently until she regained some control.

"Thanks."

"Any time." He smiled crookedly. "Not that I want to see you upset."

Lisa gave a small hiccup. "I know what you meant."

She jumped when the phone rang. Abby's door swung open, and her footsteps pounded toward Lisa's bedroom and the phone extension there. When Abby's door shut quietly, Lisa guessed she'd taken the cordless handset into her own room.

All day, the phone rang, always caught up during the first jingle. Abby didn't emerge, even for a late lunch. Bobby assured her he wasn't hungry, so Lisa had a quiet bite to eat with Joe. The bacon, lettuce and tomato sandwiches weren't haute cuisine, but neither were they pasta.

"Thanks for lunch," Joe said. His arms circled her and she turned to face him. "Ever hear of the old tradition of kissing the cook?"

She smiled as his lips descended. The outside door swung open behind her, but Lisa lingered for a moment longer.

"Yuck," Bobby said as he came in sweating and smelling of hot little boy. He wiped his face on the tail of his Royals T-shirt. "Can I have some juice? I've been drinking water all morning."

"Of course." Lisa opened the refrigerator and got down the pitcher, letting the coolness sweep over her skin for an extra moment. The recent heat wave had the heat index climbing up near one hundred. The air conditioner fought to keep the house cool.

"Can I have it outside?"

"Sure." She went to the cupboard for one of the plastic containers she used in the kids' school lunches.

"Uh, Mom?"

Lisa turned to see Bobby looking uncertain. Her eyes met Joe's, who looked as amused as she felt. "Yes?"

"Can I have two?"

She raised her eyebrows in question.

"I met a kid who just moved in down the street. We've been playing Horse. I won. He asked me could I go to his house. He got a dirt mound in his backyard."

She didn't bother to correct his grammar. "Where does he live? Wait—Bobby, is he outside right now?"

Her son nodded.

"Well, for heaven's sake, ask him in. It's got to feel like an oven out there."

"He can't. I did ask, Mom. He's not allowed unless his mom meets you first."

Lisa smiled, having the same rule for her children. "Is she home now?"

Bobby's vigorous nod almost shook his head off.

"Then what do you say we go meet her?" Lisa welcomed the opportunity. She'd just been thinking about losing touch with her old friends and needing to get out more. The mother of a boy Bobby's age could be a valuable friend, with whom she'd have something in common.

Bobby's grin showed the new gap.

"What's that?" Joe asked. "You lost a tooth?"

Bobby nodded and stuck his tongue in the hole. "See? I lost it last night when I brushed my teeth before bed. It almost went down the sink."

"And you didn't tell me until now?" Joe pretended to be hurt.

"I got five dollars from the Tooth Fairy 'cause it's my first tooth."

"No way."

The boy nodded. "The other teeth you get less for. Everybody else in my class lost some of their teeth already, but Mom said I would, too, when my teeth wanted to leave me."

Joe laughed. "Your teeth like you that much?"

"Yeah. I'm going to spend my money on something, but I don't know what yet. Mom said I don't have to save it."

He glanced at Lisa, who shrugged. "Lucky you."

She and Bobby left on their errand after Joe assured her he'd listen for Abby. He stood and stretched to release the kinks of the long plane ride the day before, followed by too little sleep. He'd been eager to get here. His attachment to Lisa and her kids should bother him more, he knew, but the happiness he'd felt seeing her welcoming smile counteracted his anxiety.

"Is she gone?"

Joe nearly jumped out of his skin. He pivoted to see Abby's tear-streaked face peek around the cabinets. "Your mom and Bobby went to meet your new neighbors."

Abby blew out a breath and came over to the table.

"Are you okay?" He didn't want to get into the middle of this, but he could hardly let the girl stand there miserable and alone.

She nodded unconvincingly.

Joe got her a glass and filled it with juice, hoping it would restore some of Abby's sweetness and energy. At the moment, a gentle breeze from the air-conditioning vent would knock her down.

"Thank you." She drank most of the glass, probably parched from her long day of crying. The redness and swelling around her eyes looked painful. "Can I tell you something?"

"Of course." Joe stopped. "It's not a secret I'd have to keep from your mom, is it?"

Abby hung her head. "She'll find out."

"Okay, then."

They sat at the kitchen table. She inhaled deeply. "At the hotel, you know, when my friends all went to that concert?"

He nodded.

"Well, they had a room next door to Sally's parents, but her parents never came in to check on them, so they decided to play Truth or Dare because no one thought about bringing a Ouiji board."

Joe held up a hand. "Slow down, Abby. You don't have to tell me all in one breath."

She gulped and nodded. "It was Sally, Lauren, Leah, Stephanie, Erica and Amy. Do you know how to play Truth or Dare?"

He nodded. "Vaguely."

"Someone asks a question and if you don't want to answer it with the truth, you have to take the dare instead. You really *have* to do the dare, too. You can't refuse."

"Okay."

"Well," Abby exhaled the word on a sigh, "Sally asked Lauren which boys she liked, but she didn't want to tell them. Probably because Sally would tease her. I think Lauren likes Steve, but she doesn't want everyone to know."

Joe smiled, lost in the world of little girls. Did eight- and nine-year-olds really have crushes on boys? Whatever happened to cooties?

"Anyway, Lauren decided to take the dare." Abby raised her tortured expression to Joe. "Sally," she whispered, "dared her to go down to the gift shop and steal something."

His breath caught.

"All the girls had to go make sure she did it. So they sneaked out of the room, and Sally's parents never knew it." Her face screwed up. "Well, not till they got called."

"Abby, I don't know what to say."

Her face crumpled as a shudder ran over her thin frame.

"It could have been me," she wailed.

Joe opened his arms, and Abby crawled onto his lap, burrowing into his shoulder much as her mother had before lunch. He rubbed her back while she cried.

"Shh," he crooned over and over. "Sweetie, it's all right."

Abby cried harder.

"You wouldn't have stolen anything. You would have said no. Don't cry now."

"You can't say no to a dare," she hiccuped. "And the ones who just went down to watch got in trouble, too. The gift shop lady called the hotel police guys."

"Oh, jeez. That must have been scary."

He felt her nod against his now-damp shirt.

"I feel bad."

"Of course you do."

"Because I'm glad it wasn't me. If Mom let me go, I'd be in trouble, too."

"You can't feel guilty about that, Abby. It's natural you're relieved."

The kitchen door opened. After a brief pause, which seemed to Joe to take forever, the door closed and the chair to his left slid out from under the table.

"Hey, guys," Lisa said softly. "What's going on?"

Chapter Ten

Lisa listened to Abby's rehashing of events as told to her through the third-grade grapevine. Most of the girls who'd gone to the concert were grounded, but word had circulated nonetheless.

"They didn't do anything wrong, Mom."

"They didn't stop their friend from stealing, though, honey. Going along to witness the act, even to verify it for a game, makes them guilty."

Lisa sneaked glances at Joe while she explained things to her daughter. He stayed silent, taking it all in. She wanted to thank him for being there when Abby needed a shoulder, literally. The bond between the two surprised Lisa, but it pleased her, too. Even though Abby had okayed her marrying Joe, Lisa hadn't realized how attached Abby had become.

His coming through so well shocked her, which in turn made her a little ashamed. But who would have thought Joe Riley would turn out to be a rock for her kids?

Unfortunately, Lisa didn't have time to concern herself with his silence now. Somehow she had to console her daughter, while at the same time enforcing the lesson to be learned through the other girls' actions.

Joe left shortly after Abby's revelations. Lisa frowned as she shut the door behind him. He'd been lost in thought as she talked with Abby. He had something on his mind and weighing heavily, judging by the frown line between his brows.

Did it bother him to have her daughter turn to him for comfort? Could he not see the gift Abby had granted him with her trust?

"HOW DID IT WIND UP with Abby?" Ginger asked later that night when Lisa explained on the phone about the concert. The kids had gone to bed; Abby subdued, Bobby exuberant about his new friend, Dean, down the block. "Did you two make up?"

"Yeah," Lisa said, "I think Abby and I will be fine. She's a little tentative around me right now. Doesn't want to admit I was right, but she knows it, which is enough."

"That's a consolation, anyway."

Lisa sighed. "I'm sure next time she wants to go somewhere, we'll get all the details beforehand, and she'll listen to my opinion."

Ginger snorted her laughter.

Lisa smiled. "Wishful thinking?"

"I'll say. But good luck with that."

After a moment's silence, Lisa confessed, "Joe went all quiet on us before he left. He didn't say when we'd see him next."

"Is that unusual?"

"No. We don't have an arrangement. He just shows up." Lisa frowned. His presence had become a habit lately.

"So," Ginger said, "if he doesn't come by in a day or so, give him a call. Invite him to dinner. If you want to be alone, maybe go to a show, I'll watch the kids."

"Thanks. I might take you up on your offer. But don't you

need your evenings free? I do have a teenager to call for babysitting," she said, thinking of Moneesha.

"Kyle doesn't mind if I go out every once in a while."

Lisa hesitated, then asked, "How's the Baby Project going?"

"We're still at it. Taking it a day at a time."

Lisa bit her tongue. Her friend's tone reflected her disappointment. Lisa wanted to ask if Kyle's attitude had improved, but blasting her husband for selfishness wouldn't help Ginger. "That sounds right."

"It's the advice we got at the fertility clinic."

"Oh? How'd that go? I didn't realize you'd have any results yet."

"Not results," Ginger said. "Wouldn't that be nice? We just talked to a doctor, a counselor, some nurses, the mailman."

Lisa chuckled, as she knew Ginger meant her to.

"Still," Ginger continued, "it helped us to step back and take a breath. The doctor had us fill out questionnaires separately, like my answers would differ from Kyle's. We have the same sex life. We didn't do any testing, if you know what I mean."

"No little cup for Kyle?"

"Exactly. Which is a good thing, considering I don't think Kyle really wanted to go in the first place."

Lisa clenched her jaw. She wanted to ask if Kyle had picked up any basic biology lessons in his thirty years.

"Let me know," Ginger said, "if you hear from Joe or if you decide to call him."

"I will, but I figure he'll just show up whenever he's thought through his problem. Whatever it is."

JOE THOUGHT ABOUT IT. Every time he had a moment's respite from his work, which he tried not to let happen too often during the next week, he thought about it.

Abby crawling onto his lap had felt like glass exploding in his chest. He wanted to wrap her small body in his arms and protect her from all the bad things that might ever happen in her life.

But how could he?

He'd encouraged Lisa to let Abby go to the concert. If Lisa had followed his advice while he played at being the perfect dad, it would be Abby the other kids were gossiping about. It would be Abby who'd stood in front of hotel security, scared and in trouble. It would be Abby whom the other parents wouldn't let their kids play with.

He shook his head at the magnitude of his failure. It was bad enough his attempts at fatherhood had flopped, but the consequences to one innocent little girl would have been disastrous.

He had to stay away from Lisa's family. Fortunately, he didn't have much influence on Lisa's decision-making, but who knew what other potentially dangerous choices he'd make? What if he'd allowed Bobby to go play at the new kid's dirt mound and the family hadn't been good people? This parenting thing lay fraught with booby traps. One wrong step and he'd ruin a life. He cared too much for Abby and Bobby to risk them.

He inhaled a deep breath, knowing what his next move had to be. He'd have to talk to Lisa. She'd wonder about his absence if he stopped coming around without explaining. Her doubting whether she still had the catering contract after the dinner at his folks' house proved that.

The catering contract. Joe rubbed his eyes, gritty from a week of sleepless nights. He'd have to see her at the company party next month, but that he could handle. It was the parenting thing he didn't have a clue about.

Later that day, Joe knocked on Lisa's door, still uncertain of the right words. Would she understand his decision?

Abby swung open the door. "I saw it was you."

Joe stepped in, trying not to be obvious about checking out the girl's appearance. Her eyes didn't glisten with tears, and no red marks blotched her face. She seemed less energetic but not forlorn.

"Mom's in the basement working. Do you want to go down or should I call her?"

"Can you call her up, or is she in the middle of something we're not supposed to disturb?"

Abby shrugged. "She's always in the middle of something. It's her job."

He nodded with a slight smile. Lisa, a workaholic? A little over a week ago, he could have teased her about it. "See if she can take a break. If not, ask if she wants me to come back another time."

"She wants to see you."

Joe gulped. "How do you know?"

"She told Mrs. Winchester on the phone. You met her the first day you came, when you were yelling at Mom."

"I wasn't yelling at your mom," he defended himself automatically. A vague memory of a thin, rusty-haired woman laughing at him as he'd hopped around holding his shin floated in his mind. He'd been focused on Lisa that day. And every day since.

"I'll go see about Mom."

Joe watched her shuffle off toward the kitchen and the steps beyond. Lisa wanted to see him? She'd discussed him with her best friend? If he'd been pursuing her to have an affair, this news would be encouraging. As it stood, however, he could only wonder how things had gotten so screwed up.

Lisa came into the kitchen just then, distracting him with her prettiness. She'd pulled her yellow-blond hair back in a ponytail, confining the silky length from falling into purple and yellow icing, judging by the sugary substance on her fingers. A tentative smile played around the pink lips which had haunted his dreams. Dressed in a tie-dyed, multicolored T-shirt and cutoff jean shorts, she appeared as sexy as his memory taunted him.

"Hi," he said.

Her gaze met his. "Hi."

The simple greeting said more than hello. *I'm glad to see you; I've missed you.* But in front of Abby, Joe knew they both tempered the rest of their messages. He, at least, didn't let his desire for Lisa creep into his tone. He couldn't, as he'd come to back out of her life. It wasn't a cowardly retreat, but a way to save this impossible situation.

"Can I call Katelyn?" Abby asked.

Lisa sighed. "Of course."

The girl scampered from the room, her mother's gaze following her.

"What's wrong?" Joe asked.

She shrugged. "Abby has become obsessive about getting news. She calls her friends every day, several times usually, to find out if the Gift Shop Girls, as they're now known, are still in trouble."

"What trouble? Surely hotel security isn't pursuing the matter?"

"No, they've been grounded by their parents. All of them except Sally." She glowered. "According to Abby's sources, Sally got 'a stern talking-to' about her choice of friends, and that was the extent of it."

"Her choice of friends?" Joe echoed. "What about daring the one girl to steal something?"

Lisa shook her head. "Wasn't mentioned, as far as the grapevine knows. And since Sally hasn't been grounded from using the phone, some of the story has come directly from her."

"She called Abby?" His tone conveyed his amazement.

"Once. Abby told her I wouldn't let her talk to Sally for a while." Lisa smiled. "I don't mind being the bad guy for a good cause like that."

"Jeez. I can see more and more why you didn't trust the Turners with Abby." Anger burned in his gut at the thought of these people being so careless of the welfare of the girls in their custody. He mentally shook himself. Thank God Lisa never listened to him.

She eyed him. "Is that why you're here, to check up on Abby?"

"No, not entirely." He glanced around the kitchen for what would probably be the last time. The cozy eating area reminded him of the times he'd shared meals here and of kissing Lisa. "Could we sit down, maybe in the living room?"

"Of course," Lisa said, frowning at him. "What's wrong?"

Joe waited until they sat across from one another. She looked so gorgeous. He swallowed, the words causing a hard lump in his chest. As the words weren't likely to get easier to say the longer he waited, he decided to just blurt it out. "I think we should stop seeing each other."

Lisa drew back in her chair, as though he'd swung at her.

He rushed on, "This thing with Abby. I'm not good at it, being around kids. I don't really need to come here to convince my folks you and I are together. They only have my word for it I'm here, anyway. You didn't want me around Abby and Bobby, and you were right."

Lisa shook her head slightly. "What are you talking about?"

"Just that I doubt I'll be around much from now on."

They stared at each other until Joe dropped his gaze. It skittered around the room, unable to settle. She watched him, her expression going from shocked to blank reserve. "I see."

From her tone, Joe couldn't tell what she saw. Probably not what he'd intended, but he didn't want to get into it now. He'd carved his escape route; all he had to do was run. Yet he sat rooted.

"What will you tell your parents?" she asked.

"We're taking a break." He swallowed. "So we can be sure of our feelings."

The disbelief in her eyes made him doubt whether the story would work. Would his mother believe it?

"So." She cleared her throat. "See you around. Or rather, I guess we won't."

"No, you will. At the party."

"Party?"

"The Riley and Ross year-end party in a few weeks. You're still catering for us. We have a deal."

She caught her bottom lip between her teeth, and he wondered if the gesture kept her from telling him where to stick his company's party.

"Right," she said. "I'm still on for that."

"Of course you are. I've invited my parents. Dylan's mom and his brother and wife are coming. Our families were a major consideration in relocating, so we decided to include them this year."

She nodded.

"This isn't easy for me," Joe said, needing her to understand.

She raised an eyebrow, and he realized she didn't care how difficult this was for him.

"Don't be like that," he said.

"Like what?"

"Cold."

She shrugged. "What do you want from me, Joe? You've made your decision."

There didn't seem to be anything else to say. She'd shut him out, not understanding the sacrifice he was making for her kids.

Feeling stiff and reluctant, Joe rose and walked out of the house, leaving Lisa in her chair staring after him.

OVER LUNCH, Lisa gathered her courage to break the news to the kids. She'd considered just letting it slide and tackling the issue when Abby or Bobby noticed Joe's absence, but that felt dishonest. She couldn't let another man just disappear from their lives without preparing them for it.

She made chicken quesadillas, a favorite of both kids, to soften them up. The crisp outsides crackled as the kids bit into them, and Lisa thought her own composure might shatter as easily if she didn't get this over with fast.

"I have something to tell you," she started.

Both faces raised to hers. Bobby had a thin string of cheese stuck to his chin, which, for some reason, only underscored his vulnerability.

"Mr. Riley came by earlier." She looked at Abby. "You let him in."

The girl nodded.

"He won't be visiting us as often. He wanted to let us know so we wouldn't worry he'd gotten sick or anything." She smiled, feeling ill herself. "Wasn't that considerate?"

"Why isn't he visiting us anymore?" Abby watched Lisa with too-old, too-intelligent eyes.

"Doesn't he like us?" Bobby asked.

"Of course he likes you."

"But he doesn't like you?" Bobby's simple question held no accusation, but still she winced. She'd explained that their father had left because he didn't want to be married to her, thinking the kids shouldn't blame themselves or feel unloved. Now it was Joe departing from their lives.

"I thought you were dating," Abby said.

Bobby swung his head toward her. "Dating?"

"Mom and Mr. Riley were supposed to go out. Alone." Tears swam in her eyes. "What happened?"

"Mr. Riley still likes all of us," she assured them, unwilling to play the bad guy again. "He just has commitments and can't be coming over all the time."

"Oh," they chorused.

They'd experienced a man putting work before them. Her heart broke even more seeing how easily they accepted her explanation.

LISA GLANCED AROUND the James Brothers Hotel ballroom, pleased Joe had decided on this smaller venue in Howard to celebrate the company's first year. She'd dealt with his secretary, Sue, as often as possible, trying to settle details by e-mail if she had to have Joe's decision on a matter immediately.

His employees had enjoyed dinner in an adjacent conference room and now began to trickle in for desserts and dancing. Lisa, in a rare telephone call to Joe, had claimed catering the latter part of the evening would make her a poor companion and suggested she not attend the dinner. Joe, quiet for an extraordinarily long time, had asked how he should explain this to his parents. She'd told him to improvise, as he excelled at making up stories. Her waspish tone carried through the phone line.

She saw now he'd followed up on her suggestion for the floral arrangements, giving the business to an acquaintance of hers. Cream roses adorned almost every surface, with freesias inserted in the displays for added scent, and Oriental lilies in variegated pinks for a touch of color. The subdued lighting lent the room an intimate atmosphere, while the background of soft piano music made talking possible. Later, the DJ would take over, but for now the entertainment remained low-key.

A quick check assured Lisa her waitstaff worked as efficiently as she'd quickly trained them. She'd hired Melinda and Julie, two college students on summer break, and she now breathed a sigh of relief to see how well they worked together. Ginger had insisted she come along to help, although Lisa suspected she came for moral support more than catering assistance. Lisa had Moneesha babysitting the kids again.

This night wouldn't end as the last party she'd catered for a Riley had, with her in Joe's arms. She sighed and, sensing the wistful nature of it, pushed the memory aside. She had work to do, in more ways than one. For, just as at the last Riley event, Mike and Alice attended, and she'd have to pretend to be Joe's fiancée again. This should be the last time. Surely by now he'd told his folks they were having a cooling-off period to be certain they wanted to spend their lives together. She shook her head. Only a man would come up with an explanation like that.

"He's behind you," Ginger hissed in her ear, making Lisa jump.

"Jeez Louise." Lisa put a hand over her pounding heart, glad she'd already set down the glass plates. "Don't sneak up on me like that."

"I didn't want him to take you by surprise."

"So you did, instead? And why are you whispering?" Lisa shook her head. "I know he's here."

"Did he inform his parents you guys are taking a break?" Ginger's mouth pursed, her tone sour.

"I hope so, but either way, I'm still his loving fiancée. We're just being cautious. His parents are here, so mind your manners."

"I wonder how his mom took it."

Lisa bit her lip, knowing Joe's tendency to coddle his mom. What if Alice had faked one of her "spells" during his announcement? "His folks should appreciate our trial separation. I told you how Alice feels about my being divorced."

Ginger grinned. "I can't wait to meet her. I didn't stay long enough last time to hear her announce your engagement. Do you think she'll get up and tell the women there's still a chance to win Joe's heart, as you don't have the ring on your finger yet?"

"Ha, ha."

"Shh, here he comes."

Lisa turned to greet Joe and the three people accompanying him. She inhaled deeply to settle her nerves.

"Joe." She smiled and reached her hands to claim his, pressing her lips to his cheek.

She forced herself not to stiffen as he slid an arm around her waist, pulling her to his side.

The way his navy-blue suit fit his body made her mouth water. He epitomized success, and her heart swelled with pride for him.

"How was the dinner?" She turned to the others. "I hated to miss it, but I wanted to make sure this part of the evening was as near to perfect as I could make it."

"Dinner went fine," Joe replied. "We kept our speeches short, so they wouldn't boo us off the stage."

Lisa longed to hug him but settled instead for running a hand down his tie, pretending to smooth out wrinkles.

Joe cleared his throat and turned to the group. "Good evening, Ginger, it's nice to see you. Introductions are in order. Everybody, this is my girlfriend, Lisa Meyer, who also catered tonight's desserts."

"Hi." Lisa gestured to Ginger. "This is my best friend and right arm, Ginger Winchester."

Ginger nodded to the group.

"Honey," Joe said, "you remember Dylan, my partner, who keeps me reined in—"

"Or tries." Dylan's warm handshake matched his smile. Lisa wondered if he knew of the pretense.

"—when my ideas get too far-fetched," Joe finished with a grin. He gestured to the other couple, a blond-haired man and a very pregnant brunette. "This is Dylan's brother, Adam Ross, and his gorgeous wife, Anne, who as you can see, are expecting their next child at any moment."

Lines of exhaustion had formed around Anne's eyes. Lisa glanced at the woman's feet, which were swollen around the sensible flats she wore. At the moment, the woman didn't glow from pregnancy as much as appear overcome by it.

"Your next child?" Lisa inquired. "So you have one at home already?"

The other four chuckled.

A glance at Ginger showed her friend studying her own shoes, and Lisa wondered if seeing a pregnant woman hurt Ginger. So far, she and Kyle hadn't been successful in conceiving.

"One?" Adam said with a grin. "No, ma'am. We have seven at home."

"Good thing my brother's a builder," Dylan said. "He can just add more rooms on to his house."

"Oh, my," Lisa said faintly. She blinked as they continued laughing.

"We get that a lot," Anne said with a gentle smile. "People just don't know what to say."

"'Get this woman a seat' is what they should say," Lisa countered. "Joe, what are you thinking, making her stand up like this?"

Adam chuckled. "Good point. You'll have to excuse us, but I really think we should find Mom and head home."

Anne frowned at him.

"We wanted to celebrate with Dylan and Joe," he continued, "but I can't let Anne exhaust herself."

"I don't get out very often," Anne said. "Babysitters, as you can imagine, aren't easy to find. We usually get two or three teenage girls at the same time. Thank goodness my mother-in-law runs a day care and can handle multiple children at once, so we can call on her sometimes."

"Because you tend to *have* multiple children at once," Dylan teased.

"We have triplets, twins and two single births." Anne rubbed her stomach. "There's only one in here this time."

Lisa met her eye. "Come show me what looks appealing, and I'll make you up a plate to take home."

Anne leaned toward Joe. "I like her."

Arm in arm, they walked over to the table with a quiet Ginger at Anne's other side. Anne pointed out a bit of everything, heavy on anything chocolate, and Lisa and Ginger went into the kitchen to wrap up the desserts from the assortment which hadn't been set out yet. Lisa included a few extras, keeping in mind the extra mouths at home. Seven? Good heavens.

Ginger stayed behind when Lisa returned to Joe's side. She made a mental note to check on her later, after Ginger had had time to herself. She handed Adam Ross the plate, almost dropping it as she spotted Alice and Mike Riley across the room.

"This looks scrumptious," Anne said. "Thank you."

Adam frowned. "Is that on your diet?"

She glared. "The doctor said I should have anything I want in these last days, and I want this. All of this."

He put his hands up in surrender. "Okay, okay. Just trying to watch out for you."

"I know, sweetie." She made a kissing motion toward him. "And when I need you to spoil my fun, I'll let you know."

"Fat chance. I didn't mean fat," he added quickly. "You're way not fat."

"You're on thin ice, Ross." But Anne's loving glance let everyone know he had nothing to fear.

Adam winked. "I'll make it up to you."

"Guys," Dylan said, "you're making us gag."

"He means a foot massage," Anne assured them, "and I'll take him up on it. It was nice to meet you. Thanks for this." She held up the container. They walked away, Adam's arm protectively around what would have been Anne's waistline.

"Oh, are they leaving?" Alice Riley asked as she and Mike joined the group. "I wanted to tell her about my friend, Margie's, daughter's delivery. It was her fourth child, and it didn't go at all well."

"They have to locate my mom in this crowd," Dylan said, "so you might be able to catch them."

"I don't think Anne needs to hear any horror stories from the delivery room, Mom," Joe said. "She's been in there often enough herself, as well as being a nurse."

"She's a nurse?" Lisa felt like an underachiever by comparison.

"She quit after the fourth baby to stay home with the kids," Dylan said.

"Have you found a wife yet?" asked Alice with a gleam in her eye.

Biting her lip, Lisa met Joe's gaze.

"Watch out," Joe said with a laugh. "My mother's a real matchmaker."

Dylan shook his head. "I'm in no hurry. I like to keep my options open."

"Good idea," Mike said. "No sense tying your—" He grunted as Alice's elbow connected with his ribs.

"If Joe or I had been married," Dylan said, "it would have been harder to move the company here because of our wives' families. So you should be thankful."

"But now that you are here," Alice countered, "it's time to settle down. Like Joe and Lisa. Although they haven't set a wedding date, news of their engagement is all over town."

Lisa didn't need two guesses to know who'd been spreading that news.

Then she paused. Alice shouldn't still be telling people that. Hadn't Joe mentioned their taking a break yet?

"You'll have to excuse me," she told the others. "I need to get back to work."

"But," Alice exclaimed, "it isn't as though you're just the hired help."

"I have new assistants," Lisa explained. "I need to keep an eye on them."

Alice nodded. "You never know about new employees. They can get up to all kinds of mischief. Some of them just stop working unless you keep them under supervision."

"They're hard workers. I don't want to abandon them in case they need my help." Lisa smiled, although her jaw tightened at the elder woman's counsel. She wouldn't have anyone maligning her staff. Alice might also spread the tale of Lisa checking up on her unreliable help, making potential clients think twice about hiring her. "They're wonderful, but this is the first occasion I've had to use them since their training."

She nodded to the rest of the group. "It was nice to see you again, Dylan. See you later, Joe."

He gave her a quick kiss.

Lisa didn't see Joe for the rest of the night, deciding to take the coward's way out and hide in the kitchen.

Joe found himself at the Meyers' front door late on a Saturday afternoon a week later. After making a stand and cutting himself off from them, he discovered how acutely he missed Lisa, Abby and Bobby.

When he'd noticed a hummingbird drinking from a hanging basket of pink flowers at his mom's, he thought how Abby would take delight in the frenzy of its wings and tiny body. He saw a man in a tattered business suit walking a chimpanzee on a body leash going down the street in downtown Kansas City, and he laughed, knowing Bobby would enjoy the story. He'd taken out his cell phone to snap a quick picture before he remembered he wouldn't be seeing Bobby to show him.

Which landed him on their porch this evening. Joe had lost count of the times he'd thought of Lisa or mistaken her for another woman on the street, in a store or across a room. He envisioned her everywhere, in fact. Seeing her at the company party had only intensified his misery as she'd held herself aloof.

So he pressed the doorbell, berating himself for his weakness. But he needed to make sure the kids knew he still cared about them. He worried about hurting their feelings. Most of July had passed without his seeing them.

Lisa opened the door. By the composure of her features, Joe guessed she'd checked who stood on her porch before answering the bell. "Joe, I didn't realize you'd be coming by."

"I didn't, either." Which sounded idiotic, but her not automatically stepping back and inviting him in tied his stomach in knots.

Or maybe it was the way she looked, so beautiful and so much as though he'd found his way home. He squeezed his eyes shut for a minute, searching for the same composure she achieved. "I've missed you. All of you, the kids, too."

She stepped back and gestured him in. "Did you want to see Abby and Bobby?"

"Yes, if that's okay."

Her hesitation, though slight, still made his gut clench. Had he convinced her he wasn't good for the kids?

"How are they doing?" he asked.

"Fine. Bobby's into T-ball season now and seems to enjoy whacking the baseball. He's not Hank Aaron, but I think he's got a lot of power." She laughed. "Listen to me. I'm sorry. I can't believe I'm bragging on him like I expect a six-year-old to hit the ball out of the park."

Joe smiled. "I bet he could. And Abby? Has she recovered from the concert incident?"

Lisa's smile faded to tenderness as she led him to the

kitchen. "Yes, she's fine. She's made Lauren into her best friend."

"Lauren the shoplifter?" He couldn't believe it. "Is that a good idea?"

Lisa stiffened. "I'm very proud of her. The other girls in their grade won't play with Lauren or invite her anywhere. She's basically being shunned. I think Abby reaching out to her is very generous."

"I guess Lauren learned her lesson, huh?"

Lisa grimaced. "Yes. Abby's friendship started out of guilt. 'There but for the grace of God' kind of thing. Sally invited Lauren to the concert after Abby couldn't go, so Abby feels partly responsible for the trouble."

"That's ridiculous."

"I agree, but their friendship has worked out well. Both girls have learned about peer pressure and are stronger for it. Being friends, they can talk about it to each other."

He nodded. "Where are the kids?"

"Ginger invited them to the park to work a lemonade stand with her for the Humane Society." She glanced at her wristwatch. "They should be home any minute."

"Lisa." He swallowed. "Do you want me to leave without seeing them? Will my being here upset them?"

Again her hesitation cut him to the quick.

"I honestly don't know. Do you plan to keep dropping in? Because I rather thought you weren't."

"I didn't plan to." He couldn't say he'd just found himself at her door, missing the three of them like crazy, feeling as though he'd cut off a body part when he cut himself out of their lives. It sounded too melodramatic.

"Then I'm sure the kids would love to see you once in a while. They'd like to know you're still their friend."

Before he could say he'd like to be her friend, and more, a car door slammed. He wondered if the kids would give him the cold shoulder, as Lisa was.

A moment later, Abby and Bobby tumbled into the kitchen through the back door, followed by Ginger.

"Mr. Riley!" the two chorused, broad smiles stretching across their tanned, sweat-shiny faces.

"Hi, Abby. Hi, Bobby." His throat closed against further words. He wanted to open his arms and wrap them in a hug but didn't think he had the right. He raised his gaze to Ginger. "Hi."

She nodded, her gaze darting from him to Lisa. "Hello."

"Mom, there was the cutest puppy…" Abby said.

"No." Lisa crossed her arms over her chest.

"I liked the cat," Bobby said. "The black one with—"

"No," Lisa said. "I told you before you went we can't have a pet right now."

Joe wondered if it was time or money forcing the decision. Every kid should have a pet. He'd gotten a dog for Christmas when he was nine. Abby was responsible enough.

He caught himself. Had he learned nothing from the concert fiasco? Why would he second-guess any of Lisa's decisions? She most likely had good reason to deprive her children of a furry companion.

"Speaking of dogs and cats," Ginger said, "I have to get home and shower this lemonade off me. We went to pet the adoptive animals after our shift ended. The sugar on our hands—" she eyed the kids with a lifted brow "—and our arms and legs—"

They both giggled.

"—made us very popular with all the critters. Fortunately, the society had set up an air-conditioned shed for viewing the pets up for adoption, but I'm still cooked."

"Thanks for taking them," Lisa said.

"Yes, thanks for asking us to help," Abby chimed in. "I had fun."

"Thanks," Bobby said after a nudge from his sister's elbow.

"I should thank you," Ginger said to the kids, "and I do. You two were wonderful assistants. Have them make you some lemonade," she said to Lisa. "They're really good at it."

Ginger nodded to Joe. "Nice to see you again."

He responded in kind, liking Lisa's friend. Having heard Lisa talk about her, he knew Ginger provided great support for her and the children.

Ginger left with a cheery smile and wave.

"Are you gonna eat with us?" Bobby asked Joe.

"Uh…" Joe glanced at Lisa, wishing he could disappear.

"You're welcome to. We're grilling hamburgers."

"I'd love it." He swallowed and held her gaze, deciding not to be a coward. "But I can't."

"You're not going to work tonight, are you?" Abby said. "It's Saturday."

"No, I…I have a date."

Chapter Eleven

Joe had a *date?*

Lisa pasted on a smile, feeling as though she might seriously be ill. Why this news should blindside her, she didn't know. Their relationship hadn't even been authentic. She just hadn't realized "cooling it" meant he would date other people.

"Mr. Riley has to go," she told the kids, ignoring his start of surprise. "It was nice of him to come see you, but we mustn't keep him from his other commitment."

"Aw," Bobby said. After intercepting a glare from his mother, he added, "Glad you came by," although the pouty tone and sad face which accompanied the remark almost canceled its sincerity.

"I can stay for a while."

"No, no. We wouldn't want to keep you," Lisa said.

"Well, bye then," Abby said.

"You can go out the back," Lisa told Joe. "Kids, walk Mr. Riley to his car."

Abby yanked open the door.

Joe blinked at Lisa. "Well, goodbye. It seems I'm leaving."

Lisa stretched her smile wider. "See you."

"We're not s'posed to leave the door open," Bobby told him.

Lisa gritted her teeth against a laugh, glad for Bobby's straightforward understanding of the rules, even though the subtleties of good manners eluded him.

The door shut behind them, and she leaned against the counter, one hand pressed to her stomach. She knew full well why the news had hit her so hard.

Somehow, at some time, she'd fallen in love with Joe Riley. If only he weren't a reincarnation of her ex, she might do something about it.

"How have you guys been?" Joe asked as the children walked around to the front of the house with him.

"Good," Abby said. "I have a new best friend. Lauren."

Her stare bored into him. He smiled. "The girl from the concert?"

She nodded.

"She probably needs a friend."

Abby's shoulders fell as tension left her body. "She's nice."

"I'm sure she is if she's your friend."

"I'm going to go call her now." Abby wrapped her arms around Joe, who hugged her in return, feeling his throat constrict.

"See you."

"Bye, Abby." He took a breath and turned to Bobby. "So what's going on with you? Do you have a new friend, too?"

The boy shook his head. "Can I tell you something? Something you can't tell my mom?"

Joe winced. "I can't promise that, Bobby. I can't keep secrets from your mom."

"Yeah, but a guy like you would understand. When I told Mom, she just said I was wrong. But she's a girl."

"Yeah, she certainly is." Joe considered. "So you've already discussed this with her?"

"I tried to."

"Okay, sport, I'll listen. But if I think your mom needs to know what you say, then I'll have to tell her. Okay?"

"I guess so."

Joe led the boy to the oak tree in the front yard, sitting with his back against the trunk. He waited for Bobby to squirm himself into a confiding position, cross-legged in front of Joe.

"It's about that mean boy at school that I had to hit."

"You hit another boy?"

Bobby nodded, eyes on the grass between them. "A long time ago, in kindergarten. That's why Mom put me in a program."

"What program?"

"Before my regular school and after it. I had to learn art and stuff. So I don't fight no more."

"Anymore," Joe said automatically.

"Yeah. Mom had to pay for it and it costed lots."

Joe swallowed. Was this what had led Lisa in desperation to take up his offer? Guilt crept up his neck.

"Anyway, I just founded out Dean, you know, my new best friend that just moved in down the block?"

"Yes?"

"His mom and Arnold's mom are friends now. And I think Dean's mom is gonna find out I hit Arnold and not let me play with Dean anymore."

"Wow." Joe blew out a breath. These kids never came with problems their own size. Everything with them was a crisis.

"So do you think I should tell Dean's mom why I hit Arnold or should I just wait and see if she doesn't find out? 'Cause I wouldn't hit Dean. He's not mean to me like Arnold."

"Do you want to tell Dean's mother?"

Bobby shook his head.

"Do you want to tell me?"

A nod.

"Okay."

After taking a deep breath of his own, Bobby raised stormy eyes. "He called me a basket."

"A what?"

"A basket. Someone who doesn't have a dad."

Joe closed his jaw on his anger.

"First, I shoved him 'cause I didn't know what it meant, but the next day he told me, so I hit him." Bobby wiped his nose on the sleeve of his T-shirt.

"Did you tell your mom this?"

"I said he called me a name."

"But not what he called you?"

Bobby eyes widened. "I can't say 'basket' to my mom."

"Right. Of course not." He patted the boy's shoulder.

"It would make her sad, and also she'd wash my mouth out with soap, which isn't good to taste."

Joe nodded. "Here's what you do. Leave it alone, unless Dean can't play with you. Then you'll have to tell your mother what Arnold said so she can explain to Dean's mother."

"I can't tell her." He looked stricken. "Can you do it 'cause you know and I wouldn't have to say it again?"

Joe met Bobby's gaze and knew he'd tell Lisa eventually. The boy worried over the injustice of losing a new friend and hurting his mother. Lisa would want to know why her son had hit the boy. Joe would like to get his hands on the kid's parents, from whom he'd no doubt misheard the term. Anger burned inside him on Bobby's behalf.

"I'll tell your mom for you," he said. "But you have to not hit anyone, no matter what."

"But Mr. Riley—"

Joe held up a hand. "I understand why you did it. I would have wanted to myself."

Bobby smiled.

"But I wouldn't have. Sometimes you have to just walk away. Sticks and stones."

"But he called me…that."

"I know, and I'm not saying that ignoring him would have been easy." He met the boy's gaze for a moment. "But it would have been right."

After a few minutes of pulling grass out of the ground and tossing it aside, Bobby nodded. "I won't hit no more."

"You won't hit anymore."

"Right. But when I get mad, can I tell you?"

"Sure." Joe recalled the brush-off he'd just gotten and wondered if he'd be around to talk to. "And you should tell your mom. I think you'd be surprised how understanding she can be."

"Even the bad word?" Bobby tilted his head, skeptical.

"Even that. Tell her first that you got called a bad name. Don't just blurt it out. Women don't like surprises like that."

LISA CLEARED THE TABLE after dinner, having excused the children to go play. She needed time alone. As she scraped plates and rinsed milk glasses, a plan of sorts formed.

Maybe it was time for her to date, too.

Just the idea made her nervous. She'd prepared the way with Abby and Bobby already by telling them she might date Joe. Being with him had awakened the desire to have a man around again. Talking, laughing, kissing. Having a strong arm to turn a crescent wrench or open a jar. Watching masculine muscles flex as they performed those tasks. She enjoyed having Joe around, which should have been a warning sign in itself.

Mind made up, she decided to appeal to Ginger. Surely she or Kyle knew someone at their workplaces looking for a date. Even though Ginger's school had recessed for the summer, she would know some young teacher needing company. A personal introduction felt less terrifying than going to a bar or library or chat room or wherever it was people met these days.

Taking a deep breath, she reached for the phone.

BARRY WAS A NICE MAN, Lisa reassured herself the next Friday night, as she forced her eyes not to glaze over. Someday he'd find a woman who would want to listen to him go on and on about his golf game and the intricacies of emerging from the sand trap. Unfortunately for them both, Lisa wasn't that woman.

Ginger's husband, Kyle, had set them up, assuring Lisa his colleague had good manners and all his own teeth. She'd taken his remarks as a joke but now thought those might be the main qualities Barry had to recommend him. Next time, if she ever dated again, she'd go with a suggestion from Ginger, who knew more what type of man Lisa found attractive.

Like Joe Riley.

She mentally ground her teeth and tried harder to concentrate on Barry's story about a bogey he shot. If she continued to date, she'd look up something about golf. Not that she planned to date Barry again, but the information might come in handy for some other guy. Someone like—

No, she berated herself. She would not think about that

man. He'd moved on, driving home the point that her relationship with him was purely business.

Barry had chosen a nice Italian restaurant she'd never been to before. Although Lisa would have preferred something other than pasta, she enjoyed the ambience, with its subdued lighting and discreet waitstaff. Unfortunately, she found her attention straying to them, critiquing their performance and wondering if the friendly, efficient brunette serving the next table over would want to pick up some hours working for Goodies to Go. She mentally cataloged her purse to recall whether she had a business card on her.

"Lisa, is that you?" a strident female voice exclaimed.

Lisa glanced up to see Alice and Mike Riley approaching her table, followed by Susan Bennington and a portly, balding man Lisa guessed was Susan's husband.

She closed her eyes. Could the night get any worse?

"It is. Lisa." Alice's gaze flew to Barry. "I'm sorry. Are we interrupting a business meeting?"

Which Lisa knew was Alice's hope, as the alternative would be unacceptable—Lisa cheating on her son.

She forced a smile to her lips, doubting it appeared genuine. "Good evening, Alice, Mike. Mrs. Bennington. This is Barry Knowles."

She left the explanations hanging, not adding qualifying tags. With any luck, no one would push the matter. Eyeing Alice Riley, Lisa held her breath, having experienced the woman's tenacity. Joe had called her a bloodhound, but "bulldog" would have described her, as well.

Mike introduced Susan and Al Bennington as old friends.

"I can recommend Lisa's work," Alice said to Barry. "She catered the Garden Society Annual Hothouse Exhibit and did a superb job."

Although Alice offered the reference as a compliment, Lisa knew full well she was digging for answers.

"And more recently," Alice continued, "she catered for my son, her f—"

"I believe you've misunderstood," Barry cut in. He smiled at Lisa, who, guessing his next words, felt the veal parmigiana congeal in her stomach. "I'm not hiring Lisa. This is a date."

Alice's face pinched as she turned accusing eyes to Lisa.

Lisa raised her eyebrows. "Joe didn't mention we're cooling it for a while?"

"He said—" Alice's hand fluttered to her chest. "He—"

"Honey," Mike said, putting an arm around her waist and peering into her face. "Don't get upset."

"I'll be fine," Alice assured him in a quavery voice. She looked back at Lisa. "He told us you two decided to take a break before you got married." She ran a hand over her temple. "To make sure you want to commit to each other for life." She glared balefully at Barry while leaning more on Mike's arm for support. "But I didn't realize a break meant you'd be dating other people."

Lisa firmed her jaw. Was this an act or was Alice really as frail as she now appeared? The convenient timing made Lisa suspicious. She wouldn't be manipulated.

"Well, we are." Lisa looked to Mike, unable to catch his eye, as his attention had centered on his wife. "It was good to see you again." She included the Benningtons in her smile. "You'd better get home and rest, Alice."

Alice's gaze focused sharply on Lisa, her diamond-blue eyes splicing into her.

Lisa smiled. "You wouldn't want to have a relapse."

"Yes, yes, good idea," Mike said. "Good to see you. Come along, honey."

Lisa watched him lead her away, with Alice throwing a murderous glance over her shoulder.

"You're engaged?" Barry asked. "Then why did Kyle try so hard to talk me into going out with you?"

Okay, Lisa thought. The night could get worse.

JOE POUNDED on Lisa's door, his feelings too riled to be contained with a polite ring of the doorbell. After his mom had called him, he'd spent a sleepless night imagining Lisa in another man's arms. He hoped the kids had gone somewhere with Ginger today. He knew how his arguing with their mother upset Abby and Bobby. He also knew he could be a good father to them. Abby turning to him when she'd been upset about the concert fallout and Bobby entrusting him with the "basket" problem had proven that. He'd been there for them with love and support, doing his best. The definition of fatherhood. Too bad he'd blown things with their mother.

But whether the kids were home or not, he was sure-to-God going to have it out with Lisa now.

She opened the door, a hesitant look in her eyes. Just a wisp of silky blond hair fell out of place, enticing him to trail his fingers across her cheek and tuck that errant strand behind her ear. His pulse pounded as he imagined the softness of her skin. His gaze strayed down her creamy throat and lingered on her breasts. Traveling back up, his eyes lingered on her parted lips, then met the apprehensive expression in her blue eyes.

She smiled a little, and just that bit of encouragement made his body tighten. Reminded of his purpose here, Joe squinted hard, trying to concentrate. He had to keep a clear head.

"Hi," she said, her tone of voice guarded.

He nodded curtly. "We need to talk."

Instead of stepping out of his way so he could enter, she leaned against the door frame. "Is this about your parents seeing me out on a date last night?"

"Damned straight it is." He cocked an eyebrow. "I don't think you'll want the neighbors hearing what I have to say."

She arched an eyebrow right back at him. What the gesture lacked in arrogance, it made up for in sheer cuteness. He tried not to smile.

"You don't have to thank me," she said. "It was—"

"Thank you?" Joe cut her off.

"You're welcome."

"Very funny. I have no intention of thanking you. Going out with that guy and being seen by my folks was nearly a disaster."

"Really?" She crossed one ankle in front of the other, drawing his gaze to the shapely calves and thighs showing beneath her khaki shorts. His eyes skimmed back up her body, and his mouth went dry.

He tore his gaze away. *Don't let her sidetrack you.* It would have to become his mantra, like "Remember the Alamo." Wait—hadn't the good guys gotten slaughtered at the Alamo?

"Really," he repeated with heavy mockery. "If you think I have anything to thank you for, you're sadly mistaken."

Her gaze cut into him. She straightened and stepped backward. "Maybe you'd better come in."

A tingle of unease swept up his spine. He reclaimed the armchair he'd used on his first visit—the mad impulse that had landed him here, his now-turbulent life enmeshed with this crazy, beautiful, sexy woman's.

Why couldn't he concentrate instead of getting distracted by her? If only he could close his eyes, shut out her allure, maybe he could finish this conversation. On a whim, he did.

But without sight, he became aware of her scent—not flowery perfume or musky cologne, but flour and…nutmeg? Cinnamon? Something good, something that made his mouth water. He swore he could hear her breathing. Without sight, he remained just as conscious of her attraction. It only took on different dimensions. Giving up, he opened his eyes to find her staring at him.

"I don't see what the problem is, Joe. You're dating." Lisa shrugged. "So am I."

What an irresistible challenge she presented. He'd like nothing better than to haul her into his arms, carry her to her bedroom and make love to her for hours. The urge to claim her as his nearly conquered his better nature.

With more willpower than he knew he possessed, he stayed seated. He framed the words in his mind, reworking the speech he'd envisioned on the drive over.

He sank back against the cushion and propped an ankle on his knee. Two could play her game.

"You told your parents we're weighing our options, right?" Lisa said. "Making sure we want to spend our lives together?"

Joe forced himself not to squirm under her glare as she somehow made this his fault. She couldn't gain the upper hand. She'd already sicced his mother on him. With the steely coolness he employed many times at the bargaining table, he said, "I did."

"So if you can date, why are you upset I am?"

"I'm not upset." A patent lie. "My mother is, however. She took to her bed last night, cutting short an evening with friends."

"That's not my doing, Joe. For one thing, your mother isn't as frail as she acts." Lisa held up a hand. "I know you don't want to believe that, but just consider how opportune the timing is on her so-called attacks. For another thing, I didn't make the decision to 'cool it.' You wanted to ease your folks into our breaking up. I went along with what you wanted, as I have done all along."

"I appreciate your sticking to the agreement," he said.

"Our agreement was a godsend to my family."

"I never said we were done."

Their eyes met.

"We have unfinished business." Joe let his intentions creep into his gaze, and knew when her eyes widened, she understood him perfectly. He wanted her.

The air sizzled. Images flashed in his head, amazing carnal visions of them entangled in passion. As if they had one thought, one brain, one body, he and Lisa sat mesmerized in heated connection, oblivious to all else. Flushed and breathless, they remained locked in silent, erotic communication.

Joe moved toward her, and the intangible thread broke.

Lisa jumped to her feet. "No." She placed a palm against her cheek, shaking her head.

"Why not?" Aroused by their passionate link, he'd need a darned good reason to turn back now.

"We don't have anything in common."

He rolled his eyes. But not being a complete idiot, he said, "We might, if we tried."

He took a step toward her.

She held out a hand to stop him, then withdrew it swiftly as he made to take it. "This is ridiculous."

He stood within touching distance. "Are the kids home?"

She shook her head no. It was all the encouragement he needed.

LISA WATCHED in a frantic daze as Joe reached for her. They couldn't. He shouldn't.

Oh, but he was.

His fingers burrowed into her hair, clasped her head and pulled her closer. If he kissed her, she'd burn up.

If he didn't kiss her, she might burn up anyway.

His lips brushed hers. Skitters of awareness danced over her skin. His tongue traced the seam of her lips, and she opened to him. Her breath rushed out almost panting. She would have been embarrassed, but Joe's breathing came just as rapidly. His heartbeat thudded against her palms.

His hand trailed over her back, sent shivers up her ribs, then settled on her breast. Lisa heard a moan—hers?—and fitted herself closer.

She forced her lids open and stared into his eyes, entranced by the desire gleaming back at her. Wanting him so much would kill her. Not going through with it would be worse.

"If you're going to stop me—" Joe's gritty voice broke through her thoughts "—you'd better do it quick."

Lisa thudded to earth. Why couldn't he keep this sudden attack of morals to himself? His scruples hadn't been too much in evidence when he coerced her into their business engagement. Why did he have to get a conscience now?

"Not that I won't stop later, if you ask me to," he continued.

"Oh, shut up," she said, exasperated. She wanted intimacy. She wanted mindless passion. She wanted Joe.

She didn't want to have to make a choice.

She'd been the responsible one, the caretaker, since she'd gotten pregnant in high school. Just once, she'd like to forget the world, close the door and let go.

Joe's eyes lit, and he smiled.

The hairs on Lisa's nape rose in warning. Before she could question him, he placed his hands on her shoulders, his mouth over hers, and pushed her back on the couch. Her anger melted away as she reveled in his kiss. Anticipation filled her like helium. She forgot questions, answers, breathing. She could only feel—his breath warm on her cheek, his tongue enticing her mouth, his hands roaming over her skin.

Her blouse lay open, but she couldn't spare more than a thought for Joe's deftness. His fingers trailed over her ribs and circled her breasts. His lips traced across her collarbone, shivered up her neck. He was everywhere except where she needed him.

She loved Joe and being with him now, like this, felt right. Even though he hadn't mentioned the word *love*—of course, neither had she—and even though they didn't have a future together—

Lisa tensed, pulling away.

"What's the matter?" Joe asked, gazing into her eyes.

She wanted to weep. The pang of loss crushed her. Why couldn't she have rationalized her behavior *after* the event? "This isn't a good idea."

"Why not?"

She pushed him and he sat up, giving her room. She adjusted her clothing, trying to ignore his rapid breathing and her own thudding heartbeat.

"Sex isn't part of the contract," she said flatly.

Joe drew back as if she'd slapped him.

She immediately felt ashamed. "I'm sorry. I meant our only relationship is our contract."

He surged to his feet and paced across the floor, stopping several feet away with his back to her. "Is that what you think of me? That I'd bought sex from you?"

Lisa winced at his growl. "No, of course not."

"Had I known you needed everything spelled out, I might have put in terms to cover this contingency."

She watched him stalk to the door, regret in every pore

of her being. She'd protected her feelings, saying the most damning, harmful words she could imagine.

Now he'd left her, probably forever. She'd completed her mission. Her heart was protected from Joe hurting her, but she'd just done irreparable damage to it herself.

Chapter Twelve

Joe studied his mom over the edge of his coffee cup. She appeared healthy enough, a fact he'd had confirmed by her doctor. He set the mug on a coaster on her end table. "We have to talk."

"About what?"

"I talked to Dr. Marks. He told me you're fine."

She nodded. "Most days I am."

"Mom, I got a full report." Which wasn't the exact truth, but Joe felt justified fudging the facts. "I know you've been pretending to be ill. It's got to stop."

"I don't know why you'd say that."

"Because it's worrying Dad, for one thing."

"I haven't…" She trailed off under Joe's hard stare. "I just wanted you to be happy."

He took her hand. "How could I be happy, thinking you're having relapses?"

She opened her mouth but didn't say anything.

"You can't set me up for dates ever again. Understand?"

"Well, of course not. You're getting married."

Joe shook his head. He couldn't think about Lisa right now. The past few days without her had been sheer hell. "No, I'm not."

"What are you saying?"

"It was all a pretense, like your fainting spells. I did it to set your mind at ease."

She narrowed her eyes. "You tricked me? You've been lying to me all this time? And Lisa was in on it?"

He grinned. "Like mother, like son."

They studied one another. Minutes ticked by.

"Let's not tell your father, okay?"

"As long as you don't manipulate him anymore."

"Joseph, we're married. I can't promise that."

"Okay," he amended, "as long as you don't fake illness to get your way. Deal?"

"Deal." She kissed his cheek. "You're a good son."

"I'M SORRY, JOE. I meant to protect myself, but I hurt you, instead. Please call me."

Lisa hung up the phone with as little hope for a return call from Joe as the previous twenty or so times she'd left him messages. The past few days, she had tortured herself for insulting him. She'd meant to push him away, knowing sex would mean more to her, loving him, than it would mean to him. Until she heard the words emerge from her mouth, however, she hadn't known just how frightened she was.

Not that she could get Joe to understand that, especially as he wouldn't return her phone calls.

The doorbell rang and Lisa's heart jumped in her throat.

"Hey," Ginger said when Lisa swung open the door.

"Oh, hi."

"Honey, what's the matter? You look awful."

Lisa grimaced.

"Sorry. Probably not what you needed to hear."

"It's okay. I'm sure it's true." She headed for the kitchen. "Let's get something cold to drink."

"Can I help?" Ginger asked. "Do you need to talk to someone?"

"Talking won't help. Unless it's to Joe," she added, "who won't listen to me. He's gone for good—or at least forever."

"You fell in love with him."

Lisa blinked, pulled out of her gloom. She leaned against the kitchen counter. "How did you know?"

"You're miserable. It's got to be love."

"That's quite an endorsement." Then Lisa noticed the dark circles around Ginger's eyes. "What's happened?"

"Kyle left me."

"Oh, my God, Ginger. Was it another woman?"

She shook her head, stifling a sob. "Because I can't have babies."

They wrapped each other in tight hugs, crying for their own losses and each other's. Lisa cringed, recalling her first thought. The problem wasn't always another woman. She may not have been enough of a woman or a wife to keep Brad, but Joe never indicated any thoughts in that direction. She'd pushed him away, fearing his eventual desertion.

After several minutes, Lisa reached for some paper napkins and blotted her eyes. "Let me find some tissues for you. They'll be softer."

"It doesn't matter." Ginger blew her nose on a napkin.

"What are you going to do?" Lisa asked.

"I guess I'm going to get divorced." Tears streamed down her face, but Ginger's voice held steady. "We've been discussing options for about a week. More testing and the like. But he left yesterday."

"And you're just now coming over?" Lisa felt a stab of guilt. Here she'd been so wrapped up in her own problems the past few days, she hadn't even noticed Ginger's absence. Usually they talked every other day.

"I needed some time alone. I couldn't believe it. I thought he'd come back." She shook her head. "But he called me this morning with the name of his lawyer, so I wouldn't get the same one. A fr-friend of ours."

Lisa patted her shoulder as tears overtook Ginger again.

They talked and drank iced tea and talked some more. The kids came back from the neighbors'. Bobby's new friend had a sister, Samantha, only a year older than Abby.

"Mrs. Winchester has had sad news, so she's staying for dinner," Lisa told the kids in front of Ginger, intentionally blocking her into a corner. "She doesn't want to talk about it, but you don't need to be upset." She smiled at Ginger. "She'll be fine."

They nodded and took turns hugging Ginger, both very fond of her. Lisa gave Ginger small jobs to do helping with dinner. The kids washed up, and Lisa sent them away until she was finished cooking, in case Ginger wanted to talk. This also allowed Ginger to do the kids' chores of setting the table and filling the milk and water glasses, simple things to keep her occupied.

After dinner, Lisa set the kids up with their ice cream in front of a movie while she and Ginger ate their desserts in the kitchen.

"Stay here tonight," Lisa said at ten, exhausted by the emotional overflow.

"I can't. I need to get used to being alone." Ginger's watery smile fooled neither of them.

"Get used to it some other time. I need your help tonight."

"My help? Oh!" Ginger put a hand over her mouth. "I'm sorry, Lisa. I forgot you're having problems with Joe."

"It's okay. I can see how you got sidetracked." She hoped her request didn't seem insensitive, given the circumstances. Ginger's situation had brought home to Lisa the gravity of what she'd done in pushing away Joe. She should be fighting for him, not worrying about him hurting her. She hadn't been able to keep Brad from straying, but Joe wasn't like her ex-husband, and it was past time she remembered that.

"I need help planning how to win Joe back."

LISA STEPPED into the restroom of the restaurant, too nervous to confront Joe without checking her appearance one more time. She smoothed her mauve silk blouse, tucking it more securely into the matching flowered skirt. Thankfully, the taxi ride hadn't produced too many wrinkles. She hoped to be riding home, to his place or hers, with Joe tonight.

She knew he desired her. If he didn't love her yet, or he hadn't forgiven her for hurting him with her harsh words, she'd have to win him over. She hadn't tried to woo a guy since the tenth grade.

She inhaled and gave her reflection an encouraging smile before leaving the room. From behind a tall display of flowers, she spotted him across the restaurant. Lisa straightened her shoulders, and headed toward his table.

Joe sat considering the menu, a glass of wine at his elbow. He wore her favorite suit, the navy pinstripe he'd had on the first time he'd come to her house.

"Hi," she said, reaching his side. Her heart thundered as he glanced up at her. "May I join you?"

"I'm expecting someone."

Lisa slid into a chair, tugging the cream tablecloth in her haste. His attitude didn't help.

He raised his eyebrows at her intrusion.

"I'll just stay till she gets here."

"Did I say it was a woman?"

She coughed. "Uh, no. Is it?"

He inclined his head.

"Well, I'm sure your date won't mind you saying hello to an old friend."

"Is that what we are? Old friends?"

The coldness of his tone burned like frostbite. "I hope so. I wanted to apologize, Joe. I'm so sorry for what I said."

He looked away.

"Did you get my messages?" She knew he must have. She'd left close to forty before giving up. "Last time we were together, I spoke hastily, nastily, to push you away."

He snorted, not quite a laugh. "It worked."

"And I'm sorry. My instinct for self-protection is strong, but I shouldn't have said what I did."

"Self-protection?" He stared at her. "What did you think I would do? Attack you in your own living room?"

"No." She laid a hand on his arm, which stiffened under her touch, but at least he didn't pull away. "I knew I was safe from you, that way. I'm just such a coward."

"Oh?"

She couldn't admit her love yet, not with his chilly attitude. "I was worried about caring for you too much."

"You concealed it well."

Why couldn't he unbend a little? "I thought if we made love, you'd know how much you mean to me."

He stared without speaking.

"I thought," she continued, forcing the words out, "when you eventually left me, I'd be heartbroken."

"What made you think I would leave you?"

"Brad did."

Joe cursed. "For the last time, I am *not* your ex-husband."

Heads turned in their direction.

Lisa smiled. "Well, everybody knows that now."

Joe's lips quirked. "Sorry, didn't mean to be so loud."

"It was all me," she confessed. "I didn't think I could hold you. I really lost confidence in myself after he left, but I didn't realize it until after I ran you off."

"I didn't run that far."

"You hide pretty well."

He turned his hand over and held hers. "You found me."

She smiled, not ready for a full confession.

"I nearly called you," he admitted. "By the weekend, I would have."

"Really?"

He nodded. "I don't give up easily when I want something."

"And you want me?" She held her breath.

"You. And the kids."

Lisa closed her eyes, thankful she hadn't totally messed things up. "I'm glad. We've missed you."

"How much?"

She couldn't blame him for wanting reassurance. "Enough to write up a new contract."

He frowned. "I don't want a contract."

She'd been thinking contract in the form of a marriage license but didn't have the nerve to say it. "So nothing formal between us?"

"No."

"What will you tell your mom then?"

"I have a girlfriend with two kids. She's a caterer."

Lisa smiled.

"I'll tell her it's serious." He looked into her eyes. "Should I add we're planning to get married?"

She nodded, tears stinging her eyes.

Joe grinned. "That's probably the worst proposal ever. I'll do it better."

"As long as you've done it, that's what counts."

He leaned forward and kissed her.

The sweetness of the caress brought tears to Lisa's eyes.

"I love you," Joe said. "I'm sorry you didn't know it sooner."

"As long as you've said it." She grinned back, feeling euphoric. "I love you, too, Joe."

"My mother will be thrilled."

"As long as she quits setting you up on dates."

"I've stopped that nonsense. You were right. She's quite a bit healthier than she led me to believe."

Lisa squeezed his hand. "You love her. Of course you were concerned."

He glanced around the room. "Speaking of Mom, she should be here by now. That's who I was waiting for, not a date."

"She's not coming."

"How do you know?"

Lisa grinned, watching comprehension dawn on Joe's face.

"She set me up on a blind date? With you?"

"One last chance at love."

He laughed. "She finally got it right."

* * * * *

*Ladies, start your engines with a sneak preview
of Harlequin's officially licensed
NASCAR® romance series.*

Life in a famous racing family comes at a price

All his life Larry Grosso has lived in the shadow of his
well-known racing family—but it's now time for him
to take what he wants. And on top of that list is Crystal
Hayes—breathtaking, sweet…and twenty-two years
younger. But their age difference is creating animosity
within their families, and suddenly their romance is the
talk of the entire NASCAR circuit!

Turn the page for a sneak preview of
OVERHEATED
*by Barbara Dunlop
On sale July 29
wherever books are sold.*

Rufus, as Crystal Hayes had decided to call the black Lab, slept soundly on the soft seat even as she maneuvered the Softco truck in front of the Dean Grosso garage. Engines fired through the open bay doors, compressors clacked and impact tools whined as the teams tweaked their race cars in preparation for qualifying at the third race in Charlotte.

As always when she visited the garage area, Crystal experienced a vicarious thrill, watching the technicians' meticulous, last-minute preparations. As the daughter of a machinist, she understood the difference a fraction of a degree or a thousandth of an inch could make in the performance of a race car.

She muscled the driver's door shut behind her and waved hello to a couple of familiar crew members in their white-and-pale-blue jump suits. Then she rounded the back of the truck and rolled up the door. Inside, five boxes were marked Cargill Motors.

One of them was big and heavy, and it had slid forward a few feet, probably when she'd braked to make the narrow parking lot entrance. So she pushed up the sleeves of her canary-yellow T-shirt, then stretched forward to reach the box. A couple of catcalls came her way as her faded blue jeans tightened across her rear end. But she knew they were good-natured, and she simply ignored them.

She dragged the box toward her over the gritty metal floor.

"Let me give you a hand with that," a deep, melodious voice rumbled in her ear.

"I can manage," she responded crisply, not wanting to engage with any of the catcallers.

Here in the garage, the last thing she needed was one of the guys treating her as if she was something other than, well, one of the guys.

She'd learned long ago there was something about her that made men toss out pickup lines like parade candy. And she'd been around race crews long enough to know she needed to behave like a buddy, not a potential date.

She piled the smaller boxes on top of the large one.

"It looks heavy," said the voice.

"I'm tough," she assured him as she scooped the pile into her arms.

He didn't move away, so she turned her head to subject him to a *back off* stare. But she found herself staring into a compelling pair of green…no, brown…no, hazel eyes. She did a double take as they seemed to twinkle, multicolored, under the garage lights.

The man insistently held out his hands for the boxes. There was a dignity in his tone and little crinkles around his eyes that hinted at wisdom. There wasn't a single sign of flirtation in his expression, but Crystal was still cautious.

"You know I'm being paid to move this, right?" she asked him.

"That doesn't mean I can't be a gentleman."

Somebody whistled from a workbench. "Go, Professor Larry."

The man named Larry tossed a "Back off" over his shoulder. Then he turned to Crystal. "Sorry about that."

"Are you for real?" she asked, growing uncomfortable with the attention they were drawing. The last thing she needed was some latter-day Sir Galahad defending her honor at the track.

He quirked a dark eyebrow in a question.

"I mean," she elaborated, "you don't need to worry. I've been fending off the wolves since I was seventeen."

"Doesn't make it right," he countered, attempting to lift the boxes from her hands.

She jerked back. "You're not making it any easier."

He frowned.

"You carry this box, and they start thinking of me as a girl."

Professor Larry dipped his gaze to take in the curves of her figure. "Hate to tell you this," he said, a little twinkle coming into those multifaceted eyes.

Something about his look made her shiver inside. It was a ridiculous reaction. Guys had given her the once-over a million times. She'd learned long ago to ignore it.

"Odds are," Larry continued, a teasing drawl in his tone, "they already have."

She turned pointedly away, boxes in hand as she marched across the floor. She could feel him watching her from behind.

* * * * *

Crystal Hayes could do without her looks,
men obsessed with her looks, and guys who think
they're God's gift to the ladies.
Would Larry be the one guy who could blow all
of Crystal's preconceptions away?
Look for OVERHEATED
by Barbara Dunlop.
On sale July 29, 2008.

HARLEQUIN

///// **NASCAR**

Ladies, start your engines!

Pulse-accelerating dramas centered around four NASCAR families and the racing season that will test them all!

Crystal Hayes could do without her looks, men obsessed with her looks and guys who think they're God's gift to the ladies. She'd rather be behind the wheel of a truck than navigating cheesy pickup lines. But when Crystal runs into Larry Grosso at a NASCAR event, she meets the one guy who could blow all her preconceptions away!

Look for
OVERHEATED
by Barbara Dunlop.

Available August wherever you buy books.

Feel the RUSH on and off the track.
Visit www.GetYourHeartRacing.com for all the latest details.

NASCAR21792

▼ *Silhouette*®

SPECIAL EDITION

A late-night walk on the beach resulted in Trevor Marlowe's heroic rescue of a drowning woman. He took the amnesia victim in and dubbed her Venus, for the goddess who'd emerged from the sea. It looked as if she might be his goddess of love, too...until her former fiancé showed up on Trevor's doorstep.

Don't miss

THE BRIDE WITH NO NAME

by *USA TODAY* bestselling author
MARIE FERRARELLA

*Available August
wherever you buy books.*

Visit Silhouette Books at www.eHarlequin.com SSE24917

REQUEST YOUR FREE BOOKS!
2 FREE NOVELS PLUS 2
FREE GIFTS!

Heart, Home & Happiness!

YES! Please send me 2 FREE Harlequin American Romance® novels and my 2 FREE gifts (gifts are worth about $10). After receiving them, if I don't wish to receive any more books, I can return the shipping statement marked "cancel." If I don't cancel, I will receive 4 brand-new novels every month and be billed just $4.24 per book in the U.S. or $4.99 per book in Canada, plus 25¢ shipping and handling per book and applicable taxes, if any*. That's a savings of close to 15% off the cover price! I understand that accepting the 2 free books and gifts places me under no obligation to buy anything. I can always return a shipment and cancel at any time. Even if I never buy another book from Harlequin, the two free books and gifts are mine to keep forever.   154 HDN EEZK 354 HDN EEZV

Name _____ (PLEASE PRINT) _____

Address _____ Apt. # _____

City _____ State/Prov. _____ Zip/Postal Code _____

Signature (if under 18, a parent or guardian must sign)

Mail to the **Harlequin Reader Service:**
IN U.S.A.: P.O. Box 1867, Buffalo, NY 14240-1867
IN CANADA: P.O. Box 609, Fort Erie, Ontario L2A 5X3

Not valid to current subscribers of Harlequin American Romance books.

Want to try two free books from another line?
Call 1-800-873-8635 or visit www.morefreebooks.com.

* Terms and prices subject to change without notice. N.Y. residents add applicable sales tax. Canadian residents will be charged applicable provincial taxes and GST. Offer not valid in Quebec. This offer is limited to one order per household. All orders subject to approval. Credit or debit balances in a customer's account(s) may be offset by any other outstanding balance owed by or to the customer. Please allow 4 to 6 weeks for delivery. Offer available while quantities last.

Your Privacy: Harlequin is committed to protecting your privacy. Our Privacy Policy is available online at www.eHarlequin.com or upon request from the Reader Service. From time to time we make our lists of customers available to reputable third parties who may have a product or service of interest to you. If you would prefer we not share your name and address, please check here. ☐

HAR08R

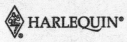

HARLEQUIN®

American ★ Romance®

CATHY McDAVID
Cowboy Dad

THE STATE OF PARENTHOOD

Natalie Forrester's job at Bear Creek Ranch
is to make everyone welcome, which is an
easy task when it comes to Aaron Reyes—the
unwelcome cowboy and part-owner. His
tenderness toward Natalie's infant daughter
melts the single mother's heart. What's not
so easy to accept is that falling for him means
giving up her job, her family and the only
home she's ever known....

***Available August
wherever books are sold.***

LOVE, HOME & HAPPINESS

www.eHarlequin.com   HAR75225

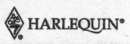

HARLEQUIN®

American ★ Romance®

COMING NEXT MONTH

#1221 COWBOY DAD by Cathy McDavid
The State of Parenthood
Natalie Forrester's job at Bear Creek Ranch is to make everyone welcome. That's an easy task when it comes to Aaron Reyes, a cowboy whose tender treatment of Natalie's infant daughter melts the single mother's heart. Falling for him would be easy—if it didn't mean giving up her job, her family and the only home she's ever known....

#1222 FOREVER HIS BRIDE by Lisa Childs
The Wedding Party
Brenna Kelly just took that fateful walk down the aisle...as maid of honor at her best friend's wedding. But when the bride's a no-show, Brenna suddenly has to cope with a runaway wedding...and her own runaway feelings for the jilted groom—handsome Dr. Josh Towers.

#1223 BABY IN WAITING by Jacqueline Diamond
Harmony Circle
When Oliver Armstrong took in Brooke Bernard as his temporary roommate, he should have known the free-spirited beauty would promptly turn his life upside down. Especially when she found out she was pregnant. Now she wants Oliver to help her round up a suitable husband. But the ideal mate is closer than she realizes—right under the same roof!

#1224 A COAL MINER'S WIFE by Marin Thomas
Hearts of Appalachia
Single, with twin boys to raise, high-school dropout Annie McKee is torn between choosing hand-me-downs and charity from her Appalachian clan or leaving Heather's Hollow and finding a better future for her boys. But the proud widow might have another option—*if* she can accept handsome neighbor Patrick Kirkpatrick's avowal that there's nothing secondhand about love!

www.eHarlequin.com

HARCNM0708